MARK H NEWHOUSE

My Family Secret: The Holocaust

Newhouse Creative Group

First edition

ISBN: 978-1-945493-44-7

This book was professionally typeset on Reedsy.
Find out more at reedsy.com

Foreword

This novel is historical fiction based on a real event, however the characters are fictional and no resemblance to real people should be inferred.

Sadly, Hitler and the Nazis were all too real. Their horrific actions are also too real and though I have taken great care in limiting graphic descriptions, parents and teachers may want to preview this work before giving it to their children. As Grandpa Sam says, "They see much worse on television."

Nevertheless, the plot deals with the real events of the Holocaust, providing an important example of the horrors that hate can create when unleashed.

My Family Secret: The Holocaust is the story of a boy who discovers that his family's secret history is not a "fairy tale with a happy ending," so please help young readers by discussing this story of love that overcomes the shadows of hate.

"Never again to anyone."

-Mark

I

LONG ISLAND, NEW YORK, 1999

I loved mysteries until I learned that my family was murdered. I must share the story, so it never happens again to anyone.

CHAPTER 1

I got up to answer the phone. Nobody ever called this late at night. Was it an emergency?

Dad beat me to the phone. "I guessed it was you," he said.

I turned back to Magnum P.I., but jumped when Dad shouted, "Why are you doing this? I keep telling you it's a lost cause."

I pretended to watch my show but something was wrong. Nobody ever ticked Dad off. He was Mr. Calm.

Dad slammed down the phone. "Goodnight son," he said, "Don't stay up. You have school tomorrow."

The phone rang again.

Dad looked at it as if it was booby-trapped and said, "I told you we'll discuss it tomorrow. It's crazy. I don't believe you want to do this." He slammed the phone down again.

"Dad, are you all right?" I hated seeing him like this.

"He wants us all to go to Poland. Can you believe it?" Dad sounded ready to bite my head off.

"Who wants us to go where?"

"Poland. This summer. It's crazy." Dad examined the phone, as if to see if he broke it. "Do you even know where Poland is?"

Why is he mad at me? I didn't do anything. What happened to Mr. Calm?

"David, it's in Europe. You should know that. That's where your Grandpa and Nana came from. It's near Germany, where I was born."

"Oh, that Poland." I remembered Poland was somewhere in Europe, which I knew is across the Atlantic Ocean. Geography wasn't my favorite subject.

We hardly talked about it in fifth grade. That was the year we did American history.

Dad gazed up the stairs. "Poland. How am I going to tell your mother? She had her heart set on Hawaii for our twelvth anniversary this summer." He climbed the steps looking like someone headed to his execution. "Good night, son. I'm sorry I lost my cool. It will work out."

I turned back to the T.V., but couldn't concentrate. Dad is an accountant and always looks at things super-logically. So why did he lose his cool tonight? Just then I heard loud voices upstairs. Mom and Dad hardly ever argue. I moved to the bottom of the stairs to hear what it was about.

It was silent again.

Good. Whatever it was couldn't be that important. I shut off the television and went up to my room. I checked my backpack to be sure I had my homework in my looseleaf. Satisfied, I shut off my lamp and got into bed.

My nightlight was out, so I climbed back out of the bed and flicked the switch. When I returned to my bed, I lay on my back and looked up at the luminescent stars Dad put up on the ceiling when I was little. Some fell down from time to time. He grumbled about the cheap adhesive as he dangled on the ladder to replace them. "Aren't you old enough yet for me to take these down," he asked each time.

"I'll never be old enough," I replied.

Dad laughed. "I wish that was true," he said.

Staring at those stars was all I needed to fall asleep. In those days, I never had bad dreams. At least, none that I remembered in the morning. I didn't know about the murders yet.

CHAPTER 2

The next morning, I grabbed my backpack and raced down the stairs. I forgot about the phone calls. I had a test on which to focus.

Mom sort of grunted at me when I entered the kitchen. She didn't have makeup on and was still in her robe. *On a school day?* Usually, she's pushing me out the door. "Hurry up, David! You'll be late for school!" Not today.

"Good morning, Mom." I got myself cereal and milk. (Mom usually has breakfast ready for me. A clue: something wasn't right.)

Mom twisted her hair, which is blond and down to her shoulders. Dad and I have curly, brown hair. She also has light freckles across her nose and cheeks while Dad and I have darker skin and zero on the freckles. It's like we're different species.

"Are you okay, Mom?" I asked, sitting at the table.

"Just fine and dandy." She poured a cup of coffee. No sugar or cream. (Another clue: Mom hates plain coffee.)

I ate my cereal, but Mom looked spaced-out. "Mom, are you sick or something?"

Mom looked over her cup at me. "Do you know what it costs to fly from New York to Poland?" She threw her spoon into the sink. It made a clunking noise. "Do you even know where Poland is?"

This time I was ready. "Poland is in Europe."

"It's in Europe," Mom muttered. She took a sip of her coffee and made a sour face. "It costs a fortune to get there."

I didn't say one word.

Mom dumped her coffee down the drain. "If I hear one more word out of anyone about Poland!" She stormed out of the kitchen, the swinging door hit the wall .

Wow! Mom never acts this way.

The kitchen door inched open.

Now what?

Dad peeked around the door. "Is the coast clear? Your Mom is in a really bad mood. Watch out, Sport." He pulled the door all the way open. "I don't blame her. She had her heart set on Hawaii this summer." He poured coffee and grabbed a jelly donut. "We went there for our honeymoon. You'd love it."

"Hawaii? Cool." I saw the waves crashing on the sandy beach from Hawii Five-O, another favorite detective show.

"Yeah, Hawaii would be cool." Dad sighed. "I never thought our family would ever go back to that place."

"Poland?"

"Yeah. Poland."

"Do they wear grass skirts in Poland?" I asked. Even Einstein, a genius, didn't know every detail about every country in the world. We never studied Poland by fifth grade. I guess it wasn't important.

Dad looked as if he'd been shot. "Grass skirts in Poland? Now I've heard everything. You're joking. Right?"

I figured I'd better say yes.

"Grass skirts in Poland. That's funny, David. I can use a laugh today." Dad gave me a kiss on the cheek. "I'll have to remember that one." He picked up his briefcase and left.

Hawaii would be cool, I thought, as I raced to catch the school bus. I figured that by the time I got home everything would be back to normal.

Boy, was I wrong.

CHAPTER 3

Did you ever have something 'buzz' around in your head and you can't stop thinking about it? I didn't think this Poland thing was important, but it kept buzzing and buzzing around in my brain. This whole situation came up so suddenly, and it was driving Mom and Dad nuts. So what was it about?

I had a few clues. Grandpa and Nana came from Poland. I knew that because Grandpa and Nana talked 'funny.' My best friend, Jeff, says Grandpa sounds like a Russian spy. (Jeff watches too many James Bond movies. I love them too.)

I like my granparents' accents. Nana is gone but sometimes, I hear Nana in my dreams. I know it's her because her 'w' sometimes sounds like a 'v.' So, 'water' sounds like 'vater,' and 'window wiper' sounds like 'vindow viper.' I guess they do sound a little like spies.

The more I thought about the phone calls, the more curious I got. Why did the calls make Dad and Mom so mad? Were they freaking out just because they wanted to go to Hawaii?

I'd seen Mom and Dad's honeymoon pictures. Hawaii looks fantastic. It has beautiful beaches, blue water and great food. And, girls in grass skirts and guys who twirl swords with fire on them. Yeah, Hawaii would have been cool. Poland? I never heard of anyone in my school who went there. Why did Grandpa want us to go there of all places? It kept buzzing and buzzing in my brain. And then, in the middle of math class, not my favorite anyway, a few minutes before lunch, it hit me. It felt like a punch in the stomach. Sometimes, old people want to go back to where they were little kids before they…before they….

I couldn't say it, but just like that, the mystery was solved. Grandpa was getting ready to 'leave' me. No. Not Grandpa too? Not shortly after losing Nana. I was afraid we were going to lose Grandpa Sam so soon after he moved back from Miami. Could it be true? Grandpa and Dad didn't always get along. Mom and Grandpa hardly spoke at all. Did Grandpa want to go to Poland because he was… dying?

I pictured Grandpa in my mind. On Hanukkah, when he visited from Brooklyn, he looked smaller. I asked him, "Grandpa, are you shrinking?"

Grandpa laughed. "You are right, Duvidel. (That means little David in Yiddish, a language nobody in our family understood except Grandpa.) "I am growing like you, only backwards. Next time I visit, I will be your size. And then, who knows?"

"Who knows?" After Nana passed away, two years ago, in Miami, Grandpa moved back to Brooklyn. He started walking with a metal cane, one with four rubber-tipped feet. He walked slow and made low groaning noises when he got up from a chair. "I need oil," he joked, but his face looked as if he was hurting. He couldn't walk far before he sounded as if he swallowed a whistle. Mom said he had asthma from something that happened a long time ago. She never explained what happened when I asked, so I figured it wasn't a big deal. It's just the way he breathed. But nobody else sounded like that.

"Holy moly! It's true." I didn't want to believe it, but the clues added up.

I didn't tell Jeff on the bus ride home. He was talking non-stop as usual. I tuned him out with all the thoughts about Poland and Grandpa now driving me nuts too. This thing was catching.

As soon as I got home, I ran up to my room and pulled my photo album from a shelf. I found a picture of Grandpa holding me when I was a few days old. He and Nana lived in Miami even then, but came up after I was born. He looked proud holding me in his arms. Seeing him like that made me smile, but we hardly ever saw my grandparents after that. I missed them, even though I didn't know them well. I wondered why Mom never got on the phone with them. Sometimes, Dad looked as if he swallowed a lemon when he got off the phone with Grandpa. Why they didn't get along was a mystery I didn't think much about.

I dug in my jeans for my ever-ready folding magnifying glass. After reading Sherlock Holmes, the world's first detective, I had to have one. I held the small lens over the picture of Grandpa. His hair was gray ten years ago, but much thicker, no bald spots. Nana was next to him. She had a pretty smile. I liked looking at her. She was a little lady. Grandpa looked serious in most of the photos. He hardly ever smiled.

I turned the pages. There were a few more pictures of Grandpa. There were hardly any of Nana. She was sick even then. And now, just when I was getting to know Grandpa....

But Grandpa's tough. I had to be wrong.

The door opened downstairs. Dad was back from work.

I stashed my magnifier back in my jeans, replaced the album, and headed for the kitchen.

Dad usually beat Mom home from her office. He'd sneak a chocolate bar from the fridge and give me half. He always gave me the bigger 'half.' "Don't tell Mom," he'd say. 'Robbing' her chocolate stash in the veggie drawer was a joke between us. Like Mom didn't know everything going on around here? She was the best detective ever. Nothing got past her.

I ran downstairs, ready to get my 'half' of the chocolate bar. "Mom?" What was Mom doing home so early?

Mom was sagged on a kitchen chair, staring at the oven. "Please, go upstairs and get dressed. Dad called. We've got company."

"That's great. Who's coming?"

Mom made a face I can't describe.

CHAPTER 4

Mom sounded as if she was sleep- talking. *Why?* And then I remembered what bummed me out all day. "Mom, can I ask you something?"

Mom opened the fridge, dug in the veggie bin, snapped off half a chocolate bar, and handed it to me. It was the smaller 'half.' She never gave me any-size snack before dinner. "Snacks ruin your appetite," she said. Something was definitely up.

Mom gave me the once-over. She had pretty light-blue eyes, not like Dad's and my plain brown ones. Her parents, and Aunt Janie, had blue eyes too. How come they were the lucky ones? I would have killed to have blond hair and blue eyes like they had. "David, is something wrong?" Mom asked.

It jumped out of me, "Is Grandpa dying?"

"What? David, what made you think Grandpa is…is…leaving us?"

She couldn't say 'dying' either. "Dad says Grandpa wants to go to Poland all of a sudden. Isn't that like a last wish?"

"Oh, I see." Mom handed me the last bit of the chocolate bar. For once I got the larger half from her. "David, don't worry. Your Grandfather is fine." She gave me a hug.

"But doesn't Grandpa want to go to Poland?"

Mom nodded. "Oh, yes. He does."

"Why?"

"Because he's crazy." Mom looked embarrassed. "I shouldn't say that about your grandfather."

I always suspected Mom didn't like Grandpa much. Did she really think he was crazy?

Mom wiped back my hair from my forehead. "You need a haircut mister," she said.

I wasn't going to let her change the subject. "Mom, what's going on?"

Mom looked as if she was thinking. "David, your Grandpa wants to go to Poland to get back some property that was stolen from him."

"Really? That's it?"

"It's crazy."

"If someone stole something from me, I'd want it back. Why is that crazy?"

"It happened sixty years ago."

"Sixty years?" *That is crazy.*

"Yup. Sixty years."

"Why'd it take so long to get it back?" If I was his P.I., (Private Investigator,) I'd get it back for him in no time. "What did they steal from him?" I asked, thinking how I could solve this case.

Before Mom could answer, Dad burst through the door and slammed his briefcase on the table. "I love him, but he's stubborn as a mule!" He raced for the stairs and the bathroom. "I think I'm getting an ulcer."

The upstairs bathroom door slammed.

"You're not the only one," Mom shouted, gazing at the door to the living room.

I jumped up when I heard, "tap, tap, tap."

CHAPTER 5

The tapping could have been a pirate's wooden leg, or a giant woodpecker. I knew who it was. *On a school night?* I ran to the living room.

"So, Duvidel, you don't have a hug for your Grandpa? I come all the way on the train from Brooklyn, and you look on me like I'm a stranger from space?"

I ran to give Grandpa a hug, surprised I was almost as tall as him.

Grandpa's metal cane stood by itself on its four rubber tips, so both of his arms wrapped around me.

"Hi Grandpa," I said, smothered in his coat. He was always cold. He said that's why they moved to Florida before I was born. I learned later the weather was only a small part of the mystery of why they left New York. It was something else they all hid from me.

Grandpa held out his right hand.

I held out mine. When he squeezed, he wasn't even as strong as when he came for Hanukkah. I was right. Grandpa was getting weaker. Shrinking and weaker? Did Mom lie to me? Was she afraid to tell me Grandpa was dying?

Grandpa smiled. "You're becoming a man, tall like your father." He plopped down in Dad's favorite reclining chair. "You're growing, or, I am shrinking again." He chuckled. "Soon you'll be a giant to your old Grandpa."

Dad sat on our couch. "He's only five-four, Papa."

"He will grow." Grandpa looked at me. "He will be six feet at least. When you was born, we didn't have much food. It was too soon."

Dad shot Grandpa a warning look.

They both got quiet, just looking at each other.

What's wrong with them? Someone say something. Did they argue in the car? They were only together for the short ride from the train station.

After I don't know how many minutes, Dad cleared his throat, and asked, "How was school today?"

"Okay." I answered like I always did. Nothing much ever happened. I was a good student and never got into trouble. That was going to change.

"What's new?" Dad took off his glasses, red pinch marks on the sides of his nose.

"I got two A's and a B+."

"Two A's? That's great! What was the B for?" Dad didn't believe in B+ but loved when I get an A+. Did that make sense?

"What is this, the FBI? So many questions?" Grandpa interrupted.

"Papa, it is a game between David and me. We do it every day."

Grandpa shook his head. "I also wanted to know what you did. Ask him one good question. David, what is the best thing what happens to you today?"

That was easy. "I hit a home run in gym for the first time ever. It was great." I didn't tell him they pitched slow for me. I was a detective, not an athlete.

"Good for you. Tomorrow you will hit two runs. Like Mickey Mantle, the greatest ball player what ever lived. Did I tell you about the time I met him? I was at Yankee Stadium—"

"That's great, David." Dad cut Grandpa off. "We'll practice more this weekend."

Grandpa nodded. "And now, my sweet Grandson, tell your Grandpa what was the worst thing what happens today?"

I couldn't tell him. I clammed up.

Dad leaned toward me. "Did something bad happen today, David?"

Grandpa's dark eyes through his round glasses looked really large. His cane was standing on its four legs by itself...the way it would if he was gone. "The worst thing that happened today is..." It stuck in my throat.

They peered at me with worried faces.

What else could I say? "Grandpa, are you going to die? Mom says you're not." *Oh my God! I said it!*

Dad nearly fell off the couch.

Grandpa said, "Are you mashugah?" (That means crazy.)

"David, where did you get that idea from?" Dad asked.

I replied, "Why do you suddenly want to go to Poland if you're not...."

"Ah, so this is it." Grandpa gave Dad a funny look. "Duvidel, your grandpa is not dying. I have some good years left."

"So, why do you want to go to Poland?"

Grandpa frowned. "It is time to get back what belongs to us."

"Papa, we agreed to talk about this later."

"My Duvidel asks now. Are you ashamed of our past?"

"Of course not. How can you say that?"

Grandpa shouted, "What does he know about our history? Does he even know our family was murdered?"

It was as if I was struck by lightning. *Murdered? My family?*

"Not now," Dad said. "Please Papa, let's have dinner and then we'll talk—"

"I want my only grandchild to know. I won't be here forever. Who will tell him? You? You didn't tell even until now."

Why was Grandpa shouting? His accent was stronger than usual. He said our family was murdered? It couldn't be true. Bad English?

"Let's discuss this later," Dad repeated. "Christine should be here—"

I smelled cherry cough drops on Grandpa's breath, or was it medicine?

"Do they teach about the Holocaust in your school?" Grandpa shot at me.

"Papa, he's only ten. Not now," Dad said.

"It's a simple question. Duvidel, do they teach about the Holocaust?" Grandpa was in my face. He was the cop and I was a criminal being scared into a confession.

I didn't answer. I was stuck on the word, 'murder.'

Grandpa snarled, "You see, they never learn this in school. It's a shame. It's a sin. Soon all of us, the last few who lived through the Shoah will be gone. Nobody will know. How can you let this happen?"

"That's not fair, Papa. Christine, and I, decided we should wait until David is old enough."

14

Why were they yelling?

Grandpa kept going, "He knows nothing about our past! Is this what should be?" His accent was very strong now. "It's my fault. No matter how my Esther and I felt about what you did, we should not move to Miami. Then my Duvidel would know about his past."

Dad aimed his eyes at me. "David, they teach about the Holocaust in school. Right?"

I didn't know the word. It sounded like, 'How low cost?'

Grandpa burst in. "I want to know if my only grandson knows what happened to OUR family? This he should know by now, if nothing else!"

Grandpa's loud voice scared me. I blurted out, "They were murdered."

Dad said, "Papa, you see, David knows. Let's talk after dinner. Like we agreed."

"Why was they killed?" Grandpa asked, shoving my father's hand away.

"I said, not now." Dad's eyes shot toward the kitchen door, which swung open. "Chris is coming. Stop. Please?"

"Dinner is ready!" Mom announced, but stopped cold. "What's going on?"

"Papa asked David about the Holocaust," Dad replied.

Mom's smile morphed into a frown. "Sam, we said we'd discuss this among ourselves after dinner."

"I told Papa that," Dad said. "More than once."

"This is more important than food." Grandpa returned Mom's look, eye to eye.

It was like x-ray vision that can melt rocks when Mom did that look. "Dinner will be cold," Mom said, not sounding very warm herself.

Grandpa gripped the armrests and rose slowly. "Your Mama says it is time to eat, so it is time to eat. Come here, Duvidel." He placed his hand on my shoulder. "You are almost a man. It is time you help your old Grandpa."

Grandpa's hand felt heavy, but I was proud he leaned on me to help him walk to the dining room. Suddenly, he whispered in my ear, "Tonight you will learn the truth. I swear, that while I am still breathing, you will know how our family was killed."

The way his fingernails dug into my flesh, did I want to know?

15

CHAPTER 6

Someone always talked at dinner in our house. Not tonight. Everyone was silent. The tension was driving me nuts. I made up my mind that I would find out what Grandpa was so hopped up about. Wouldn't you want to know if someone in your family was murdered? What kind of a detective would I be if I didn't try to solve my family's case?

At first, I thought it was Grandpa's bad English that made it sound as if it was more than one murder. A whole family? Who could get away with a crime like that? It had to be his bad English. Or so I thought.

"David, go upstairs and finish your homework," Mom said after we finished eating.

Are you kidding? Go upstairs after I passed on warm apple pie and ice cream, my favorite dessert, to speed things up, so I could hear Grandpa's story. "I did it already. Can I stay with Grandpa?" I moved next to him.

Grandpa said, "David is not a baby anymore."

Baby? I'm going to be a sixth grader next year.

"We should discuss this first," Mom replied. "David, please go upstairs—"

"I want to hear about the murders." I was tired of being sent to my room every time something cool was going on.

"Murders?" Mom glared at Grandpa. "Is that what you told him?"

Grandpa sighed. "You see. This is why he must know the truth. He thinks this is like from a police show. He knows nothing of his family history. It isn't right."

Dad took Mom's hand. "Chris, Honey, Papa may be right. We don't want him thinking we're lying."

My parents lie to me? My detective curiosity was racing full speed.

"I don't want him frightened." Mom looked into Dad's face. "Maybe you're right. I never want him to be ashamed of who he is, of his past…OUR past." She looked at Grandpa. "Okay, Sam, but take it slow."

Grandpa smiled at Mom. "Thank you, Christine." He turned to me. "David, my dear Grandson, tonight I am telling you a story. It is a true story. It will change your life, as it changed mine."

Dad cut in, a worried look on his face. "David, you need to understand, Mom and I wanted to tell you this before. We felt you were too young. We didn't want to scare you."

Why did that scare me more?

Mom sat down on the edge of the couch.

"We're all here. Go ahead, Papa," Dad said. He took my hand in his.

Grandpa's voice was softer. "David, you should know, first, our family did not always live in America—"

"I know. We're from Poland. That's in Europe, across the Atlantic Ocean."

Grandpa smiled. "Yes. Good. You, David, are the first of our family born in America."

"Mom was born here," I said.

"Yes, I forgot." Grandpa glanced at Mom. "I meant from your father's family. Your father was born in Germany, and I was born in a city in Poland called, Lodz, (pronounced Ludge in English)."

"Lodge? I never heard of it."

Grandpa shot Dad a look. "I was one of nine children, and for many years we was happy in Poland, even if sometimes things were not so good for us."

"Nine children? How come I never met any of your brothers or sisters?" This was turning into a night of mysteries. "I have eight uncles and aunts?" Why didn't anyone ever tell me that?

"They would have loved you," Grandpa said, his voice shaky.

Mom gave him a funny look.

Grandpa nodded his head slowly. "I will tell you of them a little later. Let's begin at the beginning. My father, Marek, and your great Grandpa, Isaac, worked very, very, hard in Poland. Over the years they saved some money and

17

bought a small apartment house, where we all lived together. They rented out a few rooms and made a little more money—"

"We were rich?" Mystery solved. Some crook stole a lot of money from my Grandfather and it took him sixty years to catch him. I, David the Detective, could have found him faster than that.

"Rich? No. We was comfortable only." Grandpa looked at Dad. "I thought this would be easy to tell."

"Sam, would you like coffee?" Mom was half off the couch before she finished the question.

"Thank you Christine, but coffee keeps me awake. Without my sweet Esther, I have enough trouble sleeping. So many years later I still have nightmares."

Grandpa has nightmares? Dad sometimes had nightmares. Mom told me that once, when he looked like he stayed up all night. She said he watched some movie about something terrible. She never told me what movie, only that it was a true story about something that happened a long time ago…in Europe.

I spotted Mom give Dad 'the look.'

Dad stood. "Papa, it's getting late. Let's finish tomorrow."

"You were talking about your father, Grandpa," I said quickly, not wanting to get thrown off track by Dad stopping the story.

"Oh yes, my father…the apartment building." Grandpa's hand formed into a fist in his lap. "I will tell you now what happened in our home in Poland." He glanced at Mom. "I will try not to frighten him."

The way he said that sent shivers down my spine.

CHAPTER 7

That night, when Grandpa's story was over, I couldn't sleep. I kept seeing Grandpa and hearing his voice. His face looked haunted, eyes glowing from the table lamp reflection, as he told me what happened to the family I didn't know I had.

"In school, they teach you about Hitler?" Grandpa asked.

"Who?" *Was this going to be a quiz about school?*

Mom said, "David, Adolf Hitler was Germany's ruler when Grandpa was a boy. He started World War 2."

"I've heard of World War 2," I said. "The United States won that. Didn't we?"

"I guess they didn't study that yet in school," Dad said, looking embarrassed.

Grandpa glared at Dad. "He doesn't know about Hitler?"

Dad looked at Mom, and she looked at him, and I looked at them both. "We figured we'd tell him when they started teaching about it in school; usually in sixth grade, I think. That's only next year," Dad said.

Mom jumped in. "Sam, you know Robert had nightmares as a child. He still does...like when he saw movies about it. How can you blame us if we didn't want that for David? You said you have nightmares still."

"Yes. I am still haunted by the past." Grandpa replied. "I will try to not give him bad dreams, but David should know the truth."

Mom nodded her head. (Clue: It was a slow nod. She wasn't smiling.)

The suspense was killing me. Get to the murders already, I thought, glancing at the clock on the wall.

Grandpa looked as if he was thinking of what to say. "David, Hitler was the worst man what ever lived. He should rot in hell!"

"Sam! Language!" Mom gave him 'the look' again.

"They hear much worse on television," Grandpa muttered. "Alright. Alright. But Hitler, may he rot wherever he is," he glanced at Mom, "was the Devil. David, the Devil."

With the table lamp casting shadows on his face, Grandpa looked a little like the devil too. "How come he was so bad?" I asked, unable to stop staring at Grandpa's face.

Grandpa looked at Dad. "He does not know Hitler. I can't believe this."

"He's still too young to understand all of it," Dad said, in a tense voice.

Understand all of what? What the heck is so awful? I had seen horror movies where all kinds of terrible things happened to people. How bad could this be?

Grandpa leaned forward and placed his hands on my knees. "I want you, David, to imagine an unbelievably evil man. Hitler killed six million Jews."

What? I heard wrong. "How can one man kill so many people?" Even in my favorite video games you only killed a few dozen aliens. Six million? That would be like playing one of my games for years, and years, and years.

"He also killed millions of other people," Mom interrupted, glancing at Grandpa.

"This is true," Grandpa said. "Anyone who Hitler decided was not good enough or an enemy, he murdered."

"He really killed millions of people?" I asked, not believing this was possible, except in superhero movies, when some monster wanted to destroy the world. But that was make-believe. They were saying this Hitler guy was real.

"Hitler didn't do it himself. He made others do it," Dad explained.

How do you make others kill? "Did he hypnotize them?" I asked, not understanding what this had to do with Grandpa's family.

"Yes, in a way," Grandpa said. "It was like an evil spell he threw on the German people."

"Let me try," Dad said. "Many people, non-Jews, in Germany, didn't like Jews—"

My eyes shot to Mom. "You like us, Mom. You're not Jewish."

Mom threw up her arms. "I told you he wouldn't understand. We should wait a few more months when he learns about it in school—"

"You want a stranger to teach him?" Grandpa asked. "Someone who only knows from books what I lived through?"

Mom sank back on the couch. "No. I guess not. It should come from us, his family." She smiled sadly at me. "Baby, you're right, I'm not Jewish. Your dad is, and I love him, and you. That's what matters." She looked at Grandpa and repeated, "That's what matters."

I finally got why Grandpa and Mom didn't get along. I remembered how Grandpa blew up when Dad said I wasn't going to have a Bar Mitzvah, the ceremony of becoming a man when a Jewish boy turns thirteen. It ended up with Dad screaming, "I don't care if he's a Jew or not. I don't know if I believe in God anymore."

I was shocked. How could Dad not believe in God? Why did that make Grandpa so angry?

Dad and Grandpa didn't talk for months after that argument. Then Nana died. They made up…sort of. Sometimes, like tonight, I wasn't sure. They could start arguing at any second. It sometimes felt as if we were all sitting on a barrel of dynamite. One wrong word, and bang, a big explosion. It was a mystery I couldn't solve.

"I keep telling you he's too young for this," Mom said and shot her eyes at Dad. "Why don't you say something? He's your father."

"Maybe, Chris is right," Dad said. "A few more months can't hurt."

"You can't protect David forever," Grandpa replied. "Christine, the cat is out of the bag."

What cat, I thought, as Grandpa and Mom were having a staring contest while I waited for the answers. Now, I not only had a murder to solve, (a bunch of murders by some guy named Hitler), but also had to find out who let the cat out of the bag. We didn't even have a cat!

CHAPTER 8

Grandpa broke off his staring contest with Mom. She always won with me too. "The cat is out of the bag, Christine," he repeated. "We can't go back. We should not go back."

"What cat?" I asked. "Was the cat murdered too?"

Dad sighed. "David, when Grandpa says, 'the cat is out of the bag,' he means since you already know some things about what happened, we need to tell you the rest. It's a figure of speech."

Mom nodded. "David, I love your father and you...and your Grandpa here. But the truth is, and this is hard for me to say, there are many people who still don't like Jewish people."

"I never met any," I said, but remembered something that happened a few weeks ago. I was walking home from the school bus when I saw a sixth grader, Tony, beating on a kid named Joey. I was walking away, avoiding trouble, when Tony screamed, "Drop dead, you dirty Jew!" I wanted to get out of there before Tony, or one of his goons, spotted me. As I hurried past, I heard Tony shout it again as he punched Joey. It didn't seem important at the time. I guess since I'm only half Jewish, and most of the time I forget that. I thought it was just a dumb thing kids say. Kids and grown-ups get mad and say bad things sometimes. Everyone calls people names. They don't really mean it. Nobody else did anything about it either.

Mom frowned. "I hope you never do meet anyone who hates you because you're Jewish. But Hitler knew many Germans blamed the Jews for the problems they had. He got them to do terrible things to the Jews. I hate telling you this." She looked upset.

I still didn't understand why she found it difficult to talk about. We always talked about things...other than our family.

Grandpa growled, "Hitler, he should rot, wanted to kill every one of us. He wanted there should not be one Jew left in the entire world."

I was shocked. "Why? What did Jews do to him that he hated them so much?" I couldn't imagine hating anyone enough that I'd want to kill them. "Did they do something wrong?"

Mom said, "David, the Jews did nothing wrong. Hitler was full of hate. Nobody really knows why, but some people are just like that."

Mom was on the edge of the couch, like she wanted to escape.

Dad said, "Your Mom is right. There is absolutely nothing wrong with being Jewish, Christian, Muslim, or anything else, as long as you don't hurt others."

Grandpa shook his fist. "It was Hitler. He knew if he could make people hate us, they would not fight him taking over the whole world—"

"Grandpa, he took over the world?" Why didn't I hear of him before?

"Duvidel, it is hard to believe someone is such a monster. Many people could not imagine such an evil man could become Germany's ruler." He smiled sadly. "My Papa and Mama were good people, so they could not believe anyone could be so full of hate for us. Some, thank God, did believe, and escaped to America, and other places, before the war. My parents, may they rest in peace, did not want to leave our home. We was there for many generations. It is still our home." He turned to Dad. "You should understand this. After all we went through—"

"Papa, believe me, I do understand," Dad replied.

Grandpa frowned. "My parents stayed."

"They stayed and were killed by Hitler?" This wasn't like any mystery I ever heard of before. On T.V. crime shows, one or two people got killed, but millions? All because of one man? I didn't believe it. How could I? But it was my Grandpa, and my parents, finally 'letting the cat out of the bag.'

Mom opened her mouth, about to say something.

I was afraid she was going to send me to bed, so I said, "Grandpa, you said you had eight brothers and sisters. What happened to them?"

"Another night, David." Mom lifted herself off the couch.

"They was all killed, David. All of them," Grandpa said softly.

"Enough," Mom said.

"All?" I stood and looked down at him. "Grandpa, how did you get away?"

Grandpa said, "I didn't get away. I was killed too."

At that moment, in the dim light, he looked like a ghost.

CHAPTER 9

Grandpa bit his lip. I do that when I don't want to cry.

I reached for Grandpa's hand. I thought his bad English made it hard for him to explain. It didn't make sense. How could his parents and all his eight brothers and sisters have been killed? Why did he say he was killed? He was sitting right here, with me. I was holding his hand. Bad English?

"You can't imagine how terrible it was," Grandpa continued. "We lived in the city with other Jewish families for many years. And then, Hitler's soldiers invade Poland, in 1939, and everything gets worse, as if over-night. They chase us into the ghetto—"

"What's a ghetto?" I asked.

Grandpa looked at my father. "He doesn't know?"

Mom to the rescue again. "David, a ghetto is…well, Jews were not allowed to live just anywhere once Hitler took over. They were forced to live in a crowded part of the city called a ghetto. It usually had a wall and barb-wire fences around it—"

"Grandpa had to live there too?"

Grandpa nodded his head. "It was a terrible place. A slum. Armed guards all around to keep us inside."

"Nana too?" I couldn't imagine how anyone could hate my Nana. She had such kind eyes and a gentle voice, which I still heard sometimes in my dreams.

"Yes. That is where your Nana became sick." Grandpa sighed. "You never knew what would happen. For no reason, the Germans would beat us —"

"Were they bullies?" I thought of Tony. I should have tried to stop him. None of the kids made one move to help Joey. Were they all afraid as I was? One kid couldn't stop a beating like that. Could he?

Grandpa nodded. "Yes, they was bullies. Terrible bullies."

"They beat you up just because you were Jewish?" I heard Tony screaming again, "Drop dead, you dirty Jew!" I was ashamed I didn't feel bad about that before.

"Duvidel, it is hard for you, living in America, to understand how this was. Many Germans and Poles hated Jews. They wanted what little wealth we had—"

"Who are the Poles?" I asked.

"That's what your Grandfather calls the Polish people," Dad explained.

Whenever Grandpa said Poles, I imagined tall, thin, aliens, who looked like skinny broomsticks with tiny heads. I liked my poles better, because I heard the anger in Grandpa's voice when he spoke about the Polish people. He called the Germans, 'butchers,' and 'murderers,' and the Poles, he called 'rats' and 'thieves.' He said the Poles turned Jews over to the Germans, so they could take their homes. He hated them all.

Because of Grandpa, I got to hate them too.

Grandpa's voice shook. "Hitler built a huge, secret army under the noses of the entire world. When his army takes over Poland, we Jews are the target for his terrible plans." His hands gripped the side of Dad's chair. "So many Poles hate us anyway, so what do we matter? They pick the meat off our bones like filthy rats."

"Sam!" Mom jumped up. "No more. He'll have nightmares. Is that what you want? Let's stop now—"

"I'm not a baby!" I was mad everyone was still trying to keep this from me. "Please mom?"

Dad stood. "Mom is right. You have school. We'll continue tomorrow night."

Grandpa wasn't ready to stop. "No, Duvidel, you are not a baby, but I still have nightmares about these things. So many years later, I hear the marching of the soldiers. We heard their boots in the streets. We were in our beds, hiding, wondering who they was coming for next. Who?"

"Sam, no more," Mom repeated.

Didn't he hear her? Grandpa kept going on as if we weren't there, "I still hear soldiers banging on our doors with rifles, smashing down the doors, shouting and pushing everyone out of their rooms. "Get out! Get out, dirty Jews!"

I shivered. It sounded even uglier when Grandpa shouted those words.

Grandpa continued while Mom looked at Dad. "They dragged everyone screaming to the streets. It was cold and dark. Rain or snow…it did not matter. Men, women, children…babies… poor, tiny, babies—"

"That's it," Mom shouted.

"Papa!" Dad grabbed Grandpa's hand, but Grandpa kept going, as if he had slipped back in time and was in the nightmare again. "There are loud motors. Rumbling, noisy, trucks are coming. The soldiers point rifles at us… big rifles. The Germans wear helmets black as tar that hide their eyes. They push so many neighbors, friends, up, into the trucks…terrible trucks." Grandpa's voice cracked. "I never forget these sounds…the boots, the banging on doors, the roar of trucks….the screaming and crying —"

"No more, Papa! I mean it! No more!" Dad moved me off the couch.

"Where did they go in the trucks?" I asked, unable to leave it like this.

Grandpa muttered, "Where did they go? Far away…very, very, far away… to a terrible place, where—"

"It's time for bed," Mom repeated louder. "Now Sam! I mean it!"

I wanted to hear the rest. That's not really true. This wasn't the kind of story anyone would want to hear before bedtime, or any time, but I had to know what happened. "I want to hear the end," I said, as Dad led me to the stairs, holding my hand as if I was a baby again.

"Not tonight, Sport," Dad said. "David," he added in a whisper, "Call me if you have a nightmare tonight. Don't be ashamed. I had bad dreams. I still do. Grandpa said —you heard him— that he even has bad dreams. So don't be ashamed. Okay? I love you, son." He gave me a kiss on my forehead. "Sweet dreams."

Sweet dreams? As I tossed and turned in my bed, safe in the good old U.S.A., even with my night light on I kept hearing soldiers marching. Suddenly, I heard a different sound. It was from downstairs.

My parents almost never shout, but I heard them, and Grandpa. I couldn't make out their words, but they were arguing. It went on for a long time. I couldn't close my eyes without someone shouting, waking me again. This was one of the scariest nights of my life. And I still didn't know the whole truth about the murders.

CHAPTER 10

"Did I dream the whole scary thing?" The ghostly eyes of Grandpa were like eyes from a bad dream. Then the shouting downstairs. It had to be a nightmare, like Dad had…like Grandpa had. "I'm late for school!"

I dressed quickly. I hurried past my parents' room. Dad was snoring? *Did the argument last all night? He's never late for work. Where's Mom?*

The stairs creaked, but I could have been a spy. My toes touched lightly on the rungs and skipped over the third step from the bottom. "Old Squeaky," I called it. Any burglar who came to our house would have got a surprise when he landed on that step. Dad was a good accountant, but lousy handyman.

Grandpa was still asleep in the guest room downstairs. His snoring was worse than Dad's. It rattled the walls. *How long did they argue? Everybody was sleeping in.*

A light in the kitchen.

I inched the door open.

Mom was in her robe again. *Is it Saturday? Did I sleep a whole day away?*

"Good morning, sweetheart," Mom said, and yawned.

"Are you okay?"

Mom was making my favorite, an omelet with hot dog bits and American cheese. She never made that on a school day.

"Did you sleep okay?" Mom served up the eggs and two slices of toast.

"Okay. Yeah." I didn't want to tell her that all night I heard rifles smashing in doors and people screaming. To finally fall asleep, I pretended it was from a movie, not real. Was I doomed to relive these scary scenes every night now that I heard the stories?

Mom gave me a curious look. "Grandpa didn't upset you? No nightmares?" Now, she was playing detective.

"No. I'm fine." I wasn't going to give her a reason to keep the truth hidden any longer. The real story couldn't be as scary as my nightmare.

Mom sat down and sipped her coffee. Most mornings we rushed around, getting ready to race off in different directions. Her eyes studied me as if I had changed over-night into someone she didn't know. In a way, I had.

"Are you okay, Mom?"

She yawned again. "To be honest, honey, I didn't sleep much. I kept thinking about what your Grandpa told you. It really bothered me."

"But you knew this stuff before?"

"Of course, I did. But last night I realized…well, maybe, we made a mistake." I stopped eating. "What do you mean?"

She aimed her crystal blue eyes at me and I wondered if she'd been crying. "David, Sweetie," she said, her voice velvety-soft, "You understand we…I… I was trying to protect you? I don't know if you're old enough now for this. Are you okay, really okay, after last night?"

"Yeah, fine." I really wasn't. I had more questions than ever. "Mom, how come we don't have any pictures of Grandpa's family?"

"There aren't any, David."

In my friend Jeff's living room they have a wall of photographs of his relatives. It looks nice. "What happened to the pictures?"

"Everything your Grandparents owned was taken away."

"Even photographs?"

"Everything was stolen, destroyed, or left behind, when they escaped Europe, after the war."

"World War 2?" I remembered that.

"Yes. Your Grandparents came to America with nothing."

"Why would people do such things to other people? I don't understand."

"I don't either." Mom smiled sadly. "Sweetie, the Germans tried to erase every sign of the Jews. It is a miracle your grandparents survived."

A miracle? Was it really that bad? "Is Grandpa a hero?" I asked.

30

"I'm no hero." Grandpa entered the kitchen, still in p.j.s and robe, leaning on his cane. "Good morning, Duvidel. Good morning, Christine."

"Good morning," Mom replied without smiling. "Coffee?"

"Thank you."

I always wondered why they said so little to each other. I now had some clues to that part of my family mystery.

Grandpa gave me a kiss on the cheek. "David, never say your Grandpa is a hero."

"But you lived when everyone else was killed. Doesn't that make you a hero?"

Grandpa sat down on a chair next to me. "Some would say, yes. I say no. When I go to the synagogue, and the Rabbi announces my name as one of the last living so many years from the Holocaust, they look on me like I'm a hero. They want me to speak, and explain to the children in school, what it was like. I don't like speaking about this horror, but I do this so nobody should ever forget what happened." He looked deep into my eyes. "But you know, my dear Grandson, the ones what died fighting against Hitler, they was the heroes. There were many Jews, and non-Jews, who risked their lives to fight this devil. Many died. So many. God rest their brave souls."

"Did you fight Hitler too?"

Grandpa shook his head. "I was young. I cared just to live. I fought the freezing cold, the sicknesses what killed so many... hunger, the worst hunger you could imagine. And worse than all this...terrible, terrible, fear."

"You were afraid?"

"David, I was always afraid. Night and day I was shaking with fear. How can such a boy be a hero? No, Duvidel, sad to say, I am no hero."

Just his stories scared the 'juice' out of me. I didn't blame him for being afraid, but I was a little disappointed. It would have been cool to tell everyone in school my Grandfather was a hero. But I didn't try to stop Tony from beating up on Joey. Maybe 'hero' didn't run in this family.

Mom placed her hand on my shoulder. "That's not true, Sam, and you know it." She looked at me. "David, your Grandpa isn't telling you the truth. He wasn't much older than you, but he risked his life smuggling food, medicine,

31

and messages to help others in the ghetto." She placed a cup of coffee and a plate of toast with glistening honey in front of Grandpa. "Think if you could have done that. I don't know if I could. He was very brave."

"So, you are a hero," I said, thinking I was lucky not to live when Hitler was around. Even Tony had been too scary for me. Imagine trying to stand up to Hitler and his army?

Grandpa looked at me with tired eyes. "If you call being a starving, scared, rat, running in stinking sewers a hero?" He shrugged his shoulders. "That is all I did. I ran through the disgusting sewers like a rat."

"You would have been tortured or killed if the Nazis caught you," Mom said. "Robert always tells me how proud he is of you."

Grandpa looked as if he was going to cry. "Robert tells you this? I am proud of him too." He swallowed hard and said, "But does it make me a hero when a sewer rat survived when so many much braver was killed fighting that devil?"

"You sound sad that you lived, Grandpa," I said, finding that very strange. I would be happy to be alive after such a terrible war. I don't like even thinking of feeling pain or dying someday. That's why I didn't help Joey when he was being beat up. I was just glad it wasn't me.

"You are a smart boy," Grandpa replied. "Sometimes, I am sad, very sad. I think this is how many of us who survived feel." He took a bite of his toast. "We feel guilty, even ashamed, we lived when so many died." He sipped his coffee. "It is hard to understand, David. You are grateful you lived through this horror, but wonder, for the rest of your life, why God chose you, and not somebody else." He sighed. "I wonder this all the time. For sixty years, I ask why God saved me. There were many better, many more religious, more worthy. Why did God save me?"

I didn't know what to say. Why did God choose him? And then I knew. "Grandpa, God chose you, so we could live."

Grandpa's eyes glistened.

I hated seeing tears in his eyes. The table shook under his trembling hands.

Grandpa smiled. "You are right, my brilliant grandson. You and your father...and mother here, are the reason God let me live." He gave Mom a quick smile and she smiled back, for once. "David, God could not let them wipe out our family. So, yes, I had to live."

"Oh my gosh! I'm late for work!" Mom jumped out of her chair. "You're a bad influence on us, Sam." She gave Grandpa a quick kiss on the cheek.

I never saw her do that before.

Grandpa looked surprised too.

"And you, young man, you're going to be late for school," Mom scolded.

"I want to hear what happened." *Not another delay?*

"Tonight." Mom gave me a kiss. "Your Grandpa is not going anywhere. I promise."

"You better not," I shot at Grandpa. "I want to hear the end of the story."

Grandpa shrugged. "It is not one of your fairy tales, with happy endings."

I knew that already. Part of my growing up was learning that not all stories have happy endings.

CHAPTER 11

When I watched mysteries on T.V. I pretended I was a detective and tried to guess the killers before the sleuths did. This mystery was real, and about my family. Grandpa said his relatives were murdered. I still didn't understand.

It's tough to keep a secret when it's buzzing around and around, so I finally broke down and had to tell my best friend. Maybe Jeff could help.

Jeff was chewing gum, as usual, when I sat next to him in the rear seat.

I waited until the bus took off. The motor sound would hide my words from nosey-bodies. "Jeff, you gotta hear what I discovered last night—"

"Not another one of your dopey mysteries? What did you find this time, a missing sock in the washer?" He laughed and then blew a bubble.

Missing sock? I couldn't wait to see the look of shock on his face. I whispered, "My family was murdered."

Jeff almost choked on his gum. "Jacobs, you idiot. That is the sickest thing you've ever said." He stuck the gum on a piece of tissue and shoved it in his pants pocket. (Mom would kill me if I did that.)

I leaned closer. "I mean it. My Grandpa's whole family was murdered."

Jeff replied, "I wouldn't mind if someone whacked my crazy older sister. I'd even give them my Space Attack games. Interested?" He burst into laughter again. "You're sick."

How could I expect him to understand? I didn't. "Jeff, listen, I'm trying to tell you my Grandpa's whole family was killed—"

"Yeah, right. Who killed them?"

"Grandpa didn't tell me exactly, but he is tonight."

CHAPTER 11

"So, Jacobs, how do you know they were killed?"

"Grandpa told me. Dad brought him over last night and they were arguing until late about it."

"You just said he didn't tell you. Make up your mind."

"He told me part of it. Every time he's ready to tell me the rest, Mom and Dad stop him. They say it's too scary. Isn't that weird?"

"Sounds fishy to me." Jeff was 'fishing' around for something in his backpack. "Your Grandpa's English is terrible. He sounds like a Russian spy. Maybe, he didn't say it right."

I felt like punching him. "Grandpa's English doesn't count when I heard him say, 'murder.' He says they were murdered by a bad guy named Hitler—"

"Never heard of him."

"He was the mean ruler of Germany. You must have heard of World War 2?"

"Oh. That guy with the funny moustache? I saw a show about him on T.V. once. But that war happened a long time ago. I leave the room when my father watches shows about war. I don't like them. Why did it come up now?"

"Grandpa wants to take us to Poland. That made Mom and Dad mad. They planned on going to Hawaii this summer."

"Poland? Isn't that in Europe? I'd rather go to Hawaii too."

He knew where Poland was? I didn't know until all this came up. "Grandpa says his whole family was killed there."

Jeff shook his head. "Your Grandpa's crazy." He leaned closer. "I seen those numbers on his arm. You know, those blue numbers."

A bell went off in my head. I'd forgotten about the numbers on Grandpa's arm. When I was little I thought all grandpas had them. I figured it was how God kept track of who got which grandpa. I'd forgotten all about those numbers since Grandpa always wore long sleeve shirts the few times I saw him since he came back from Florida. "You know, I always wondered what those numbers were for. Thanks a bunch for reminding me."

"Those numbers are from the crazy house," Jeff continued. "It's like the numbers you see on guys in jail. They got them on their suits, not on their arms. I think it's from the nuthouse, because no matter how much you try,

35

you can't take them off… like if you escape." He had a smug look on his face like he was positive my Grandpa had been in some mental institution and that's where he got his number tattoo.

I once asked Mom why Grandpa had numbers tattooed on his arm. She said it was so he wouldn't forget something. I thought it was his phone number or bank account. He was kind of forgetful. I am too. Mom says I'd lose my head if it wasn't attached to me. Maybe Grandpa would lose his phone number if it wasn't on his arm.

"Yep, if anybody did anything crazy, like killing someone, my guess is it was your Grandpa. That's how he ended up in the nuthouse." Jeff sat back in his chair. "That would also explain why you hardly ever see him—"

"Stop it! Grandpa was never in a crazy house," I said, disgusted I could think such a stupid thing for even a second.

Jeff asked, "Want a cupcake?" He held up a foil-wrapped cake crushed from being in his backpack. (He knows I'm not going to eat anything he hands me with his dirty fingernails.)

"No, thank you. Can we stick to the topic?" I was grossed-out by him mangling the cupcake in his wide-open mouth.

Jeff wiped his lips with his sleeve. "Okay, you say no nuthouse, but how else can you explain the numbers? Maybe he was in prison. He probably killed his whole family himself," He said through crushed cupcake. "Carol, my step-mother, says you never know about people. She should know. She's been married two times. I think she killed her first husband and nagged her second one to death. What a life. I got a mean step-mother and a crazy sister. Maybe your Grandpa killed his wife too?"

"No way," I said too loud. "You're an idiot!" Some kids looked at me, so I lowered my voice. "My Grandpa could never kill anyone. He loved Nana. You're the one who's crazy." I turned away or I might have punched him for this crap he was saying about Grandpa.

Jeff tapped on my arm.

"What?"

He gave me a sly smile. "What clues do you have?"

"What do you mean?" .

36

"To the murders. You say your Grandpa is innocent, so you've got to have evidence. Show me the clues."

"You're an idiot." I turned my back on him again. What clues did I have?

Grandpa said he lost his eight brothers and sisters, but he never mentioned them before. Of course, we hardly saw him until he moved back to New York, last year. Mom did explain why we had no pictures of any of them. Did I buy her explanation? Mom and Dad lied before, so could they be hiding something now. But what? What could be worse than what I already heard?

Grandpa said the murders took place in World War II, in Poland. That was long ago and far away. He said they were killed because they were Jewish. People don't kill millions of people just because of their religion. Do they? Just thinking about that was too scary. There had to be another reason. But, didn't' Tony scream, "Drop dead, you dirty Jew?" This was really confusing. I would have loved to drop this case, but it wouldn't let go. All these questions were buzzing around in my brain. Buzz, buzz, buzz.

What other clues did I have? The numbers on my Grandpa's arm. They might only be from a prison, or some nut-house, like Jeff said. Could he be right? No way! My Grandpa was as normal as me. Then why didn't Mom and Dad get along with him? Maybe he had been a hero in the war, but that didn't mean he could not do something wrong and get sent to prison. Grandpa, in prison? No way. My head hurt.

"We're here," Jeff announced. "Want to hang out on the playground? We can talk some more about your murders. I still say your Grandpa must have been a criminal. Or spy! He could have been a Russian agent. What else could it be? He talks like Dracula. "Velcome to Transylvania. I vant to drink your blood.'" He burst into hyena laughter.

And this is who I want to help me? "No. I've got stuff to do," I replied. I was mad at Jeff and more curious than ever. I couldn't wait another day. What if my parents decided I really was too young? I'd never find out what happened. I made up my mind. I'd show everyone I wasn't too young. I'd make Grandpa, Mom and Dad, proud of me when I revealed to them all of our family's dark, dark, secrets. I'd be a real detective, and surprise them all, when I solved this mystery by myself. It seemed like a good plan at the time.

"You coming or what?" Jeff asked, shoving the cupcake wrapper in his jeans pocket with the gum wrapper. (Where does he have room for all this junk?)

"Maybe later." I headed toward the rear entrance of the building.

"Keep out of trouble," Jeff shouted.

Who me? I never get in trouble.

CHAPTER 12

I left Jeff on the playground. I was in full detective mode after his stupid going on about my Grandpa in the nuthouse. I was going to crack this case wide open before I got home from school. How difficult could it be to find out about someone who killed millions of people? He must be the most wanted person on Earth. By the end of the day, this case would be solved and all would be back to normal.

I waited until the safety patrol was distracted by some kid running along the sidewalk and snuck through the glass doors in front of the stairway. Kids aren't allowed in the building before the first bell, but nothing could stop David, the detective. Or was I a spy? I switched them all the time.

I raced silently up two flights of steps and pushed open the door to the second floor landing.

The sun bounced off the glass door, blinding me for a few seconds.

There was a noise. It came from the far end of the hall. Someone was back there.

I couldn't see who it was because of the sun's reflection, but now, on a real murder case, I didn't want to be caught by my enemies lurking in the shadows. (Mom said I had a good imagination.)

Flat against the wall, I inched in the dim light to the library. If my entire family had really been murdered, there was no telling how many enemies we still had or what torture they would unleash on me.

Okay, my imagination was definitely running wild. With all that happened, was that really a surprise?

Calm down. My pulse was racing. I never broke any school rules before.

The firing squad would be nothing compared to what Dad and Mom would do to me if I got arrested for this. I thought of turning back. Did Sherlock Holmes quit just because he was afraid of being punished by his parents? Did James Bond quit even after being tortured? *David Jacobs does not quit.*

I pulled at the library door.

Luckily, it wasn't locked and opened with only a tiny squeal.

I ducked inside.

Someone rushed by. *Who is that?*

"Escaped you again, evil Dr. H.!"

The top enemy agent's weapon, disguised as a large push broom, swished past the doors.

Talk about watching too many movies! I listened at the door for the broom to swish back.

I waited to be sure the evil Dr. H. pushed his broom out of range and then turned to the bank of computers lined up in two neat rows at the far wall.

I didn't dare switch on the ceiling lights. I headed for the computer farthest from the door. I would be hidden by the other computers. All the screens faced the teacher desk. Mrs. Blake, the librarian, trusted no one. I was beginning to feel the same. *Trust nobody. Don't get caught. Don't get caught.*

I sat on the blue plastic chair and shoved my backpack as far under the table as it would go.

The computer droned like a bee as it came to life. I lowered the screen's brilliance… harder to see if someone looked through the door. My body would block most of the light from the screen. I thought of everything.

I typed in my password from home: "Sherlock007." (I bet you can figure out how I came up with that.)

No luck. This was going to be more difficult than I thought.

I typed my school code numbers. I wouldn't be able to stay on long or my numbers would give me away. They might anyway. I decided to take the risk.

The screen flashed and then stopped at the school search engine called, "School Search Engine." What genius thought of that?

I gazed at the white box and typed in, "Samuel Jacobovitz," my Grandpa's real name. Thank goodness Dad changed our last name to Jacobs. He said nobody in America could spell it or say it. Grandpa didn't like that Dad changed our name. "It sounds too Jewish for you?" he complained, starting another argument. Some things were starting to make sense.

The computer whirred like forever, and then the response appeared on the screen.

"NO MATCH."

My Grandpa wasn't famous, like a rock star or the President, so why would he be listed?

I thought for a second, then typed, "H-o-l-l-o-w-c-o-s-t." It sounded like Halloween.

The computer took its time and again said, "**NO MATCH.**" But instantly added, "**Do you mean, Holocaust?**"

I spelled it wrong? Well, it is a tough word, even for a smart ten year old. It's definitely not on my weekly spelling lists. I bet Einstein probably couldn't even spell it when he was a kid, and he was the smartest guy in the whole world.

I moved the cursor to, "Yes."

The screen flashed to an entry with the word, "**APPROVED,**" written above it in large green letters. I never saw a label like that in the few times I used the new machines. It was strange. I read the short entry below the banner. I'll warn you. It was difficult to understand:

The Holocaust, or Shoah, is what Jewish people call the period during World War II (appx. 1939-1945) when the Jews, and other groups deemed 'undesirables' were systematically exterminated by the ruler of Germany, Adolf Hitler, and the Nazis (National Socialist Party). Hitler exploited the latent antisemitism of the German and other European peoples, to establish a network of concentration camps throughout Europe, where it is claimed more than six million Jews were brought to work for the German war effort, and/or systematically exterminated. Additional undesirables, estimated at six million, were similarly incarcerated and exterminated, or caused to die by deprivation. Disease under these inhuman conditions also took a massive toll. The concentration camps were liberated in 1945, ending this gruesome episode in genocide.

References: See Hitler, Adolf; World War II; United States History/World War II; Auschwitz, genocide...."

The list of references went on and on, ending in a note, written in large red letters, at the bottom of the page:

WARNING: Access to files this subject requires administrator approval. Directive 345.423.54, Regulations, B.O.E. 1/28/54

Is that all of it? It was such a tiny box of text. Grandpa made the Holocaust sound like a big deal, but how could it be that important if all the information was contained in one paragraph? That was less than the entry for almost anything I studied in school.

I glanced at the wall clock. I was running out of time. I read the entry again, working to figure out what the hard words meant. I came to the word "gruesome." I didn't know I was dealing with something this short entry warned was "gruesome." That word was used right before the word "monsters" in some of my horror magazines, as in, "My friend, Jeff, is a 'gruesome monster' when he chomps cupcakes."

Another word stuck out from the article: 'exterminated.' It was used three times in the short entry. Jeff's father is an exterminator. Jeff told me his dad kills bugs and rats. So what did that word have to do with my family and all these people the article said were 'exterminated?'

The article mentioned the number, 'six million,' before the word, 'Jews.' That was exactly what Grandpa said: "six million Jews were killed by Hitler." I didn't believe it last night. Who would? How could anyone kill that many people? But the entry said it was true.

I stopped at the phrase, 'systematically exterminated.' What did that mean? And what did the article mean about a 'network of concentration camps?' The only camps I knew were summer camps, where some of my friends went. So what did 'camps' have to do with the killing of six million Jews and millions of other people?

"This is too tough," I muttered staring at the 'warning' about needing approval to get more information. Why the secrecy? My parents said they wanted to protect me, but why did anyone need 'extra approval' to read about the Holocaust in school?

I read the entry again until I got to 'gruesome.' It was like a stop sign. I couldn't get it out of my head. My parents, teachers, maybe every grown-up on Earth, even this computer, were hiding something 'gruesome' from us. It had to be something so horrible they didn't want us to know about it. That's why all the security. But what could be so horrible? Was it that millions died? That was horrible. But I suspected there was something else I didn't know. I needed to keep looking. But where? What was that guy's name?

I typed, 'Hitler.' In a few seconds I stared at the photograph of a man in soldier's uniform. I knew it was Hitler from his angry face, and his strange-looking moustache that looked like a black toothbrush under his nose. He looked as if he was glaring right at me.

What was really scary was his hand was raised in a salute as what looked like millions of soldiers marched in front of him. They were all giving him the same salute. "They're robots," I muttered. I didn't like this photograph. It was as if all the people were really robots, or zombies, hypnotized, marching before their leader standing high above them...like a god...an unfeeling god... a mass murderer. "He killed millions of people," I heard my Grandpa's creaky voice say. I looked at Hitler's face again. His eyes were alive, staring at me with blazing hate. He was screaming, "Drop dead you dirty Jew!"

I flipped off the photo. I was shaking with fear. Dad said Hitler talked the Germans into killing millions of innocent people. Looking at that awful picture of thousands of marching soldiers obediently saluting their evil leader, I can't explain why, but I was frightened. This really was too scary. Mom was right.

I took one more chance. To satisfy Jeff, I typed, "numbers on arms."
NO MATCH
I was about to type, 'concentration camps,' when I heard a tiny squeal. The library door opened.

CHAPTER 13

I was trapped. There was no place to hide. Who was in the library?

"What are you doing here?" The evil Dr. H. demanded, his broom-weapon aimed at my sneakers.

I couldn't run past him. His gargantuan body, dressed in tan coveralls, was a wall between me and the door.

"No kids supposed to be up here before the bell," Dr. H. said.

Dr. H, the dark-skinned, black-bearded, sinister spy, who spoke Spanish-mixed English, had me in his broom sights. No escape.

"Library monitor," I stammered, hoping he would let me go. Enemy spies with foreign accents are always dumb in the movies. All I had to do was keep my cool.

Dr. H. looked around. "Senora Blake no up here. So you are not permitted to be here. What is your name?"

"David. I'm her library monitor. She says I can come up without her." I kept hearing someone say, "Bond. James Bond, license to monitor."

"David. What is your last name?" He took out a tiny note pad from his pocket and was writing with a pencil stub, a disguised poison dart gun. These foreign spies are notoriously clever.

"Jacobs," I said softly. Maybe he wouldn't hear.

"So, how you spell this?"

"I didn't mean anything bad by being here." I didn't want him to report me to the Principal. I'd heard rumors about how our 'boss' treated bad kids. "I really am a library monitor."

He gave me the 'once-over.' "I believe you, but there are kids who do not behave. They steal and do other bad things. You understand? I must report you or I lose my job."

I didn't want him to lose his job so I spelled my name. "I'm really sorry. I won't come up early again, but I had something really important to do."

He looked concerned. "Is everything hokay? Is something wrong?"

I was scared of getting into trouble so I blurted, "My family was murdered."

"Que dices?" The broom crashed to the floor with a sound like a gunshot. "What did you say?"

"Oh gosh! I don't mean now," I said, picking up the broom. "A long time ago…in the war." I was afraid I gave him a heart attack, the way he jumped.

"Gracias a dios! I think you mean now. I am ready to call police." He took the broom. "You frighten me. Dios mio! You must not say things like this." He put the pad in his shirt pocket. "I am hokay now. Por favor, explain what you mean."

I could make a getaway. I might be able to outrun him, but he had a good look at me. Maybe I could outsmart him. After all he was just a janitor. I didn't think you had to be very smart for that job. "Sorry. I didn't mean to scare you."

Dr. H. frowned. "So what is this about? You know you should not be here without Señora Blake. Si?"

I thought of lying, but my intuition told me the truth might be the only way I could avoid being suspended, or expelled. If he took me to Principal Robinson, I was a dead-duck. Everyone knew how tough he was. My parents would have a cow if he called them. "Do you know about World War 2 and a guy named, Hitler?" I asked, thinking of a way out of this mess.

"Oh, si." Dr. H. looked surprised. "Spain, where my family comes from, before going to Mexico, was bombed by Hitler. He was a bad man, evil. But what is this to do with you?"

So, Mr. Hernandez knew about Hitler. That guy even bombed Spain. "That's what Grandpa says too. He says Hitler was the devil. He killed his parents and his eight brothers and sisters."

Mr. Hernandez looked shocked, and then, out of nowhere, asked, "Are you Jewish?"

Why did he ask that? Is he one of the people who hate Jews? I nodded, unsure I could trust him. "I'm only half Jewish. Mom is Christian."

Mr. Hernandez nodded his head. "So digame, David, why are you up here? Why would a good boy, I think you are, break rules?"

"Do you hate Jews?" I asked. Like anyone would admit that.

"No. De cierto, no. Of course not." He took off his cap which made him look a little friendlier.

"Mom says a lot of people still hate Jews. I don't know why."

Mr. Hernandez smiled. "The same reason why much people think everyone who speaks with a Spanish accent is stupid. They don't know better." He gave me a look like he knew I had been one of those people. "David, I see nothing about you I should not like. But tell me, what is it you want on the computer? I see you are using one."

I explained to him I was trying to solve the mystery of how my family died, but found very little to help.

Mr. Hernandez frowned. "I am truly sorry for your family. I understand how you feel. It is sad to learn such things. You have many questions still."

Mr. Hernandez sounded as if he cared. "Thank you. All I want to know is what really happened. I was trying to figure it out myself, to make Grandpa proud of me. I didn't think about the trouble I could get in."

"You have a difficult problemo, mi amigo. That means, my friend." He twisted his broom handle. "I think it is good for you to know this. But you must be more careful. You should not break rules."

"I've never been in trouble before."

"I believe you, David." A strange look appeared on his face. "Come with me. I want to show you something."

The way he said that made me nervous again. "I should be here when Mrs. Blake comes," I replied, wanting to remain in the safety of the library. Until a few minutes ago, he was a stranger, the mysterious, evil, master spy. It was too soon to trust someone I hardly knew.

Mr. Hernandez frowned. "I will show you an important clue to your mystery." He was waiting by the door. "This thing makes me very angry." He held the piece of paper with my name on it in his hand.

46

Was there a chance if I followed him that he wouldn't report me? Should I trust him? He had called me, amigo, my friend. Was that really enough to follow a stranger?

CHAPTER 14

I didn't know what to do. Mr. Hernandez was a school janitor, so I only saw him when he worked around the building. I never talked to him before. From his name I figured he was Spanish, but the truth is, I didn't think about him at all, not until I got in trouble. I admit it. I didn't think a Spanish-speaking custodian could be very smart. Just like he said, I was fooled by his accent and his job.

Still thinking he might not report me, I followed Mr. Hernandez, aka Dr. H., Enemy Master Spy, out of the safety of the media center, into the hallway. A few teachers were in their classrooms. I hoped one would come out and rescue me from his evil clutches.

Nobody came. I was on my own.

We were in the north wing of the second floor. Last year, I was a fourth grader here. Soon, it would be crawling with kids. I was safe. Teachers knew me.

Mr. H. stopped by a metal door in the far corner of the hallway. A sign said in large red letters, "Emergency Exit."

"We're not allowed to use these stairs," I said, as he reached for the door handle.

"You are hokay with me," Mr. Hernandez replied, as we headed down a dimly lit staircase I was never in before.

When we got to the first floor, Mr. Hernandez pushed open the heavy door.

We were in the back of the building, behind the gym. Nobody around. Nobody.

I tried to remember what Grandpa said about pretending to be unafraid. I wasn't brave like him. Time was moving slow. *Where's the morning bell? Where are the kids? Come on, let them in already?* I stopped at the door. I wasn't going to take one more step.

"Come with me. Don't be afraid. Is hokay." Mr. Hernandez gave me a smile.

I guess my being scared showed. I tried to smile back. I followed a short distance behind him.

Mr. H. talked as he walked, which made it harder to understand everything he said. "When I was a boy, your age, my parents tell me many times what Hitler did to their village in Spain. The many bombs he drop from airplanes and how the Germans kill so many innocent people. I never forget. It was terrible what he did, destroying with many bombs. He did not care who dies… men, woman, children…all the same." He looked at me. "If a man does not care who he kill, he is diablo. He is devil."

Mr. Hernandez sounded like Grandpa, but his voice was softer, more like Dad. "Hitler, he build a secret army, many tanks, ships, and more bombs and airplanes than all the world together." He stopped by a steel door. A big sign in red letters said, "OFFICIAL USE ONLY."

"I'm not allowed," I said. Where was he taking me?

"You are with me," he replied.

There was no window in the door. What was on the other side?

Mr. Hernandez searched a large metal ring that held a hundred keys. "It was a sin what Hitler do. So many die. He was a sick, evil, man."

"Grandpa says Hitler wanted to take over the world," I muttered, wondering why Mr. Hernandez was taking me through a forbidden door. "I really should go back," I said.

"Is hokay, David, mi amigo. I show you something you must see."

"I really should go."

"Ah, si," Mr. Hernandez said, placing a key in the lock.

Did the door lead to a hidden dungeon, a cell where he kidnapped kids like me, kids stupid enough to trust a stranger?

I breathed a huge sigh of relief when I saw we were outside, by the playground. There were kids waiting for school to begin.

"Is here." Mr. Hernandez pointed at the wall just outside the door.

Did he drag me all this way to look at a wall?

CHAPTER 15

A s if this case wasn't scary enough, I was in back of the building with a custodian I hardly knew. *Please, bell, ring?*

Mr. Hernandez shook me awake with his voice. "Is terrible. Look at what the bad ones, they put on my clean wall." He pointed his finger.

Why was he so angry about graffiti some kids spray-canned on the brick wall? I saw this junk everywhere. It's mischief some teenagers did.

"This one is very bad." Mr. Hernandez pointed to a large symbol in thick black paint.

I saw this weird shape plenty of times before but never bothered to ask what it was. Why should I care? I'd never do anything like this. Total waste of time and I could get in big trouble for defacing property. Dad would kill me.

Mr. Hernandez looked at me. "You do not know what this is?"

I shook my head. *Why doesn't the bell ring already?*

Mr. Hernandez said, "This is a *swastika*. It is the symbol of Hitler, the monster. All his soldiers and flags have this." He pointed to several copies of the symbol on the brick wall. "I hate when I see this disgusting thing. I clean and clean and it comes back."

I remembered this symbol all over that awful picture of Hitler and his 'robot' soldiers. I mumbled, "You see these things everywhere. I didn't know what they were." At least until I saw that photo, and even then, I thought it was just a part of their uniform. It looked almost like a cross.

Mr. Hernandez frowned. "I show you this because is a clue to understand what happened to your family. It is happening even now, David, mi amigo."

51

"Now? Dad says the war happened a long time ago." That photo of Hitler and the marching soldiers on the website wasn't even in color. It had to be really old.

"This is why I show you these ugly things. Hitler, he died long time ago. This is true. But David, the hate he tells… the hate he used to hurt, kill, so many people… this is still alive. This swastika, he spread all over. It is here, even in America, a land I love." He looked very sad. "You understand?"

"I didn't think it was important," I said.

Mr. Hernandez took a handkerchief out of his pocket and wiped his brow. "Why this symbol spreads all over the world, this evil and hate…that is what you must learn. It is because of what is happening today, that you must find the answer to your problemo. You understand?"

I didn't really, and was still suspicious of him. "Why are you helping me? Are you Jewish?"

Mr. Hernandez shook his head. "Do you think monsters like Hitler only hate Jews?"

"They don't?" Grandpa acted as if the Jews were the only ones Hitler hated, the only ones he murdered. But I remembered Mom said he also killed millions of other people.

Mr. Hernandez spit on his hankie and rubbed it on the black marking. "No good. She sticks." He glared at the wall. "It is true Hitler kills half of all Jews in world. Terrible thing. He also hated many others…anyone who he decide is 'different.'"

"Mom said he killed them too."

"Yes. He killed millions of others." Mr. Hernandez gazed at the sky and then at me. "At night you see stars. Si? So, imagine a million stars. Is a lot. No?"

"That is a lot," I agreed, grateful Dad didn't have to hang a million stars on my ceiling.

"Imagine now six million stars."

"I can't. It's too many. Grandpa said six million Jews were killed." That was a large, unbelievable, number in my mind before, but Mr. Hernandez helped me see what six million lives meant. It's like seeing the sky filled with stars, six million of them, and, suddenly they're gone. It was as if a giant eraser washed all those stars away. I couldn't believe something like that actually happened. "So many people were killed? Really?"

"Yes, David. Catholics, handicapped, gay people, any other people Hitler hated were killed. A terrible tragedy. Si?"

"I don't understand it."

"David, I have lived forty years and I can't imagine twelve million stars, or twelve million any thing. But that is how many, and more—nobody knows for sure—how many people die because of this evil man. They die because of the hate he spreads…a disease." Mr. Hernandez raised his fist at the swastika. "I hate this symbol that lives so many years. I wash this off many times. They put it back. Over and over it comes back."

I was afraid of how angry Mr. Hernandez looked. It was like Grandpa's face when he spoke of Hitler. "Mr. Hernandez, did Hitler murder your family too?"

"Hitler kills someone from every family."

"I don't understand—"

"It is hard for a young boy to understand, but everyone lost someone they loved in this terrible war. Porque? What was it for?"

"I don't know."

"David, mi amigo, it was for nothing. Nada. A waste. Such a stupid waste." The bell finally rang.

I had to go but Mr. Hernandez was talking, "I do not understand why people hate other people. I don't care if you are Jewish, white or black or anything. You are a good boy David. That is what I see. That is what is important."

Mom and Dad always said that's what they care about too. But what about Grandpa? How can he be good if he is full of anger? Mom and Grandpa are both good, so why can't they get along?

I didn't have to be a detective to solve that mystery. I now understood it was difficult for my grandparent's when Dad married Mom. They found it painful to accept Dad marrying a non-Jew after all that had been done to our family because we were Jewish. But Mom never did anything to hurt anyone.

Did she deserve to be punished for what others did? That isn't fair. Or is it?

I stared at the ugly swastika on the wall. My life was a lot easier when I didn't know anything about the Holocaust. Mr. Hernandez said, "It changed everyone." It sure changed Grandpa when he told his story.

The late bell rang.

"I really have to go, Mr. Hernandez," I said, seeing the stragglers heading into the building.

Mr. Hernandez unfolded the paper on which he had written my name. "David, yours is a most important mystery, my new friend. It is perhaps the most important mystery you will ever solve in your life."

I felt as if he was my friend. I was so scared of him before. Now that I knew him just a little, I saw Mr. Hernandez was a good, kind, and smart man. How could I have been so wrong about him?

Mr. Hernandez crumpled up the piece of paper and threw it in the trash can. "Go to class, David. Work hard so there is no more hate in this world."

"Thank you, Mr. Hernandez," I said, amazed he wasn't reporting me. "Can I come and talk to you again sometime?"

Mr. Hernandez smiled. "Any time, mi amigo. But do not break rules again. Si?"

"Si. I mean, yes."

As I waited for Mrs. Blake at the media center, I opened my notebook. So I wouldn't forget what it looked like, I drew a copy of Hitler's black symbol on a loose scrap of paper.

That was not a smart thing to do.

CHAPTER 16

Disaster struck at lunch. For once, it wasn't the cafeteria food.

"So did you solve your latest case, oh great detective?" Jeff asked, as I was chewing my indigestible square slice of pizza. It tasted like cardboard coated with a thin layer of cheese and ketchup.

"I'm working on it."

Jeff leaned closer. "Did you find out why your Grandpa has numbers on his arm? Was he in the nuthouse?"

"I told you he was not in any nuthouse. You make me crazy!" I grabbed my notebook off the table.

Jeff stared at the sheet of paper floating to the floor.

Unfortunately, he wasn't the only one who saw it.

"What is that?" Mrs. Goldstein, a sixth grade teacher asked as she swooped up the page. "Who does this belong to?"

Jeff stopped eating. He looked as if he'd seen a ghost.

I could have stayed silent, but I didn't want anyone to get into trouble. Besides, it was only a drawing. "It's mine, Mrs. Goldstein. It fell out of my notebook—"

"Come with me," Mrs. Goldstein said. "Bring your lunch with you."

How could I eat? I tossed it in the trash barrel.

Jeff was still staring open-mouthed.

Mrs. Goldstein was silent as a coffin, my coffin, as she led me into the hall. She held up the paper. "This is yours? Do you know what this is?"

"Mrs. Goldstein—" I wanted to tell her I was half Jewish, so it didn't count.

"Answer my question, please?" She shook the paper in my face. "Did you draw this?"

"Yes, but—"

"I have to get back inside before all pandemonium breaks loose. Principal Robinson can deal with this." She hurried me toward the office.

"Mrs. Goldstein, you...you don't understand." I was so terrified I could hardly speak.

"Sit here until Principal Robinson sees you. I have to get back."

"I'm sorry. I was trying to find out what it means."

Unfortunately, Mrs. Goldstein, looking very upset, rushed away.

I got stuck sitting on the office wood bench most of the afternoon. Kids looked at me as if I killed someone. I was never sent to the Principal before. I had no idea what was going to happen. All the time I was on that hard bench, I thought how solving this thing was getting me into a heck of a lot of trouble. First, with Mr. Hernandez, and now with Mrs. Goldstein. What was Dad going to say when Principal Robinson told him I was walking around with a Nazi symbol in my notebook? Not even James Bond could get out of this mess.

"You can go in now, Mr. Jacobs," Mrs. Branch, the secretary said. "I haven't seen you here before." She frowned. "Good luck."

Good luck? This was bad. I dragged myself to the Principal's open door as if I was about to face a lion in its lair.

The room was dark. It really was like entering a lion's den.

Principal Robinson looked huge, staring at me from his desk, my drawing in his hand. I can never draw anything, but this thing I draw right? What was I thinking?

"Close the door behind you, please," Principal Robinson said. His voice was deep but calm, a killer's voice.

He doesn't want anyone to hear me scream, I thought, pulling the door closed, sealing off all hope of escape.

Principal Robinson didn't ask me to sit, so I stood in front of his desk as he studied me with eyes that looked like they could boil eggs. I was glad his big desk was between us. This was getting worse by the second. Whatever made me think a ten year old could be a detective?

Seconds ticked by really slow. Why didn't Principal Robinson yell at me? It was like waiting hours for him to say something. Anything. The silence and suspense were worse.

"Do you know what this is?" Principal Robinson's voice was silky, not raised at all. It sounded scarier that way, like killers in gangster movies, calm and cold, right before they unleash a hail of bullets into your gut. This was bad.

I nodded, too frightened to speak. This was Hitler's fault. Even sixty years later, he caused trouble.

"Did you draw this?" Mr. Robinson held up the paper which now looked like a death symbol. Mine.

"I'm sorry," I tried to say, but no words came out. I nodded again.

Principal Robinson stood. He was really tall, and his skin was black and shiny, which made his eyes look more scary. He removed his suit jacket and rolled up his sleeves.

Oh my God! He's *going to paddle me!* Everyone said principals paddle bad kids. I wanted to say something, but this guy was huge. I'd never been this close to him before, and being in trouble, really deep in, made him seem even larger.

"Why did you draw this?"

Holy mackerel! He was taller than Dad, a lot taller! He looked like a football player. I was shaking. Would I make it to my eleventh birthday? I was never in this much trouble before in my entire life. POLAND! That darn place was driving everybody nuts.

"Don't be afraid," Principal Robinson said. "I don't remember seeing you in trouble before, so I'm guessing there must be a good explanation for this."

I took a breath and in one rapid-fire sentence blurted out the whole story of how my Grandfather told me my family was murdered, and I was out to solve the mystery, and the drawing on the piece of paper was a clue. I never knew I could say so much in one breath and run-on sentence. But this was my one chance to save my butt from his paddle.

Mr. Robinson didn't smile. He kept looking at that stupid sheet of paper.

I didn't move a muscle, trying to keep from passing out. Why didn't he yell at me? I finally dared to look up at his face.

He still wasn't smiling.

My eyes searched the dimly lit office for the notorious paddle. I tried not to think of what a paddle on my behind would feel like. It couldn't be as bad as I imagined. Could it? He wouldn't dare paddle me. Would he?

CHAPTER 17

I was really scared. Why did Principal Robinson roll up his sleeves? Why was he looking at me so hard? What was he going to do to me? Do Principals take 'scare' lessons?

I could almost feel the paddle on my butt. I wondered if Mom, so worried about protecting me from the story of the Holocaust, would protect me from being paddled because I drew Hitler's stupid symbol? Unbelievable! This was the worst mess I'd ever gotten into, by far.

"How old are you, David?" Mr. Robinson interrupted my thoughts. He was reading a paper from a manila file on his desk. "You're in 5th grade?"

"I'm ten, Sir...almost eleven, Sir." Did he need this information before my execution? *James Bond, master spy, about to be executed by paddle.*

"I see you get good grades. There are nice comments on your report cards too. Your teachers like you." He read another sheet in the file and looked up again. "You've never been here before? In my office?"

I shook my head. "No, Sir. Not ever. Sir."

"Please sit down." Mr. Robinson pointed to a chair in front of his desk.

I plopped down on the red, leather seat, eager to protect my butt from the deadly paddle. I looked for it, suspecting it was lurking in this office, a 'chamber of horrors,' according to rumors. Of course, I never listen to rumors. But everyone knows you don't get sent to the Principal's office, or else.

Mr. Robinson put the folder on his desk. "David, I really don't think you meant to do anything wrong here. Am I correct?"

"No, Sir. No, Sir. I never get in trouble." Except breaking into the media center, using the school computer illegally, and now this. All in one day!

"I see that from your files." He picked up my drawing again. "You know this drawing you made is called a 'swastika.' David, Swa-sti-ka." He gave me a deep look like Dad does when he wants to be sure I understand something. "Did you know this swastika is one of the most hated symbols in the world?"

I nodded.

"But you drew it anyway?" He leaned forward. "I guess you admitted that to Mrs. Goldstein so nobody else would get blamed?"

"Yes, Sir." He figured that out. A point in my favor?

"Well, from what I gather from your file, I believe you when you say you drew it to try to remember what it looks like…for further research?"

"Yes, Sir." *He believed me. What a relief!*

"It's actually kind of amazing how something like this can cause so much trouble. Isn't it?"

"I didn't mean to upset Mrs. Goldstein. I can apologize to her."

"Do you know why she got upset?"

"She's Jewish, like me, so she hates it."

"Well, that's part of it. Mrs. Golstein lost family in the Holocaust and still gets upset about it."

"I'll definitely apologize to her."

"Good. I'll talk to her too. She's a very good teacher, a very caring person. Lunch duty can be a zoo at times. I think you caught her at a bad time."

"Thank you, Principal Robinson." This was not as bad as I thought it was going to be. I imagined much worse. I died sitting on that bench, thinking of what was going to happen to me. I scared myself silly.

"David, it isn't just Mrs. Goldstein and your family who hate this. I do too."

"But, Sir, you're not Jewish. Are you?" Mr. Hernandez said he didn't like the swastika because of what happened in Spain, but Principal Robinson wasn't Jewish or Spanish. Why did he hate it?

"Do you understand what a symbol is?" Mr. Robinson asked.

"Isn't it like the American flag?" I hoped I got one question right on this butt-saving quiz.

"Very good. The Statue of Liberty, the Liberty Bell, and the flag are good examples." He pointed to the flag standing in a corner of his office. "When you say the "Pledge of Allegiance", you are swearing that you care about our country which the flag symbolizes."

"So when you draw a Swastika—"

"The people who preserve Hitler's symbol hate Jews, Blacks, immigrants, gay people and anyone else who isn't exactly like them."

"Just like Hitler," I said.

"Exactly. Now you know why Mrs. Goldstein got upset."

"Like my Grandpa." What would Grandpa Sam say if he saw me carrying a swastika in my notebook?

"Like many people," Mr. Robinson replied. "Most good people hate that symbol."

We were talking like we were friends. He wasn't going to paddle me. What a relief! But, suddenly, I thought of something much worse than being paddled. I was afraid to ask. "Principal Robinson, are you going to tell my parents?"

He didn't answer.

Oh God, he's going to tell them! I'm dead. I am so dead.

"You're never doing anything like this again. Are you?"

"Heck no! I'll let someone else solve my mysteries from now on."

"Mysteries?" Mr. Robinson looked puzzled.

It came out of my mouth like air rushing out of a balloon. I told him everything I learned so far, everything except about Mr. Hernandez. I didn't want to get my new amigo in trouble, even if I got paddled. Suddenly, I'm brave? "Please don't tell my parents? I'll never do anything wrong again. I give you my word."

"David, calm down. You've never been in trouble before. I don't think there is any reason for me to tell your parents about this incident. I think you should tell them yourself though. You should ask your parents and Grandfather to help you solve this 'mystery' before you get into more trouble. Will you promise to do that? You should always trust your parents. They love you. You will tell them?"

"I will. I promise I will. Thank you. Thank you so much."

"And David, one more thing...."

I knew it. I was about to be punished. I'd face the paddle like a man...like my Grandpa. "Yes, Sir, Mr. Robinson."

"I'd like you to come and see me when you have the whole story. I'd really like to know what happened to your family."

"You would?" Was this a Principal trick? Everyone knows they go to a special Principal school so they can learn all these 'tricks' to make kids' lives miserable.

"Yes. Maybe one day, you and I can share stories about our family histories. My great grandmother was a slave in Mississippi."

"Really? That's awful." Wow! I never would have guessed someone so smart could have come from slaves. Of course, I never thought a janitor could be smart either. It's like Mom always says, "You can't judge a book by its cover." I guess I did that a lot without realizing it. Maybe, it's just what people do.

Mr. Robinson nodded. "Grandma used to tell me terrible stories about slavery. That's why I understand what your Grandfather feels. It's easy to stay angry when people hurt those you love. I'll tell you a secret. For a while, I was angry at all white people for what slavery did to my family."

Principal Robinson didn't like White people? I was very nervous about asking him anything else, but thought he could help me with something buzzing in my mind. "Grandpa hates the Germans, and Polish people too, for what they did to his family." I never hated anybody before Grandpa told me his story. I didn't like how it made me feel now. "Is he wrong to hate them?"

Mr. Robinson glanced at his clock and stood. "I'm sorry, David, I'd love to talk more with you. Unfortunately, I have a few real 'troublemakers' to deal with before school ends. I think that's something you should talk about with your parents and your grandfather."

"I will. Tonight, I'll get all the answers." I got up, hoping he was really going to let me leave and this wasn't some kind of trick. "Thank you, Principal Robinson, for not getting me in trouble with my parents."

"You just remember to come see me after your family helps you solve your mystery. Now go to class before everyone thinks I paddled you."

He knew what I was afraid of? I was super-eager to leave, but my dumb curiosity got the better of me. "Principal Robinson, can I please ask you one last question? I promise I won't tell anyone."

Principal Robinson looked puzzled.

"Do you really paddle bad kids?" I thought I could ask, now that I was standing at the door and my bottom was safe.

He gave me a big smile and replied, "What do you think?"

I thought he didn't, but was glad I wasn't going to find out, the hard way.

CHAPTER 18

"You're alive!" Jeff gushed when I got on the bus just before it took off.

"Just barely." I was still recovering from my scary afternoon. I came really close to big trouble. I couldn't believe I got out of it. Twice in one day!

Jeff got so close I smelled gum on his breath. "What happened? I thought Robinson was going to whip your butt for sure with his paddle after Goldstein saw that thing. Don't you know what that is? Who carries that in their notebook? You're nuts!"

"Whoa! Jeff! Slow down! You know what it is?" I was surprised he knew about the swastika, or said he did.

"Oh yeah! A wrestler on cable T.V. wore one of those black ugly things and my Dad went nuts. He always goes nuts when he sees guys on motorbikes wearing that or those Nazi helmets."

"But your dad isn't Jewish. Why would he get mad about that?"

"Dad's Grandfather was an American pilot in World War 2. His plane got shot down over Germany. He hates anything that reminds him."

"Wow! I can't believe something that happened so long ago is causing so much pain and trouble today. It's everywhere, even sixty year later, and I didn't know anything about it."

"Yeah, it is kind of weird." Jeff got quiet, rare for him.

I thought of how I was going to tell Mom and Dad everything that happened to me today.

Jeff tapped my arm. "I've been kind of a pain," he said. "I thought you were joking around about your family and all. You tell those awful jokes. I'm sorry I didn't believe you."

"That's okay. I didn't believe it at first. It's a lot to swallow."

Jeff smiled. "So what now, Sherlock?"

"Nothing. I'm going to wait for Grandpa tonight. Being a detective on this case is too dangerous."

"You're giving up? That's not like you."

"Hey, I almost got paddled in Principal Robinson's 'torture chamber.' (I'd play it up big for Jeff.) Mrs. Goldstein is mad at me. I was scared to death by Mr. Hernandez, who, by the way, is a really smart guy, and a good friend." I shrugged. "I guess something good came from all this. But this Holocaust stuff is way too tough."

"But you still don't know why your Grandpa has numbers on his arm." Jeff leaned closer. "I still say it's because he was in the nut—."

"Jeff, if you don't stop saying that, I'm going to put you in the nuthouse! Or better than that, I'll get Ginny 'Brace-Face' Johnson to give you one of her big, juicy, kisses. So, shut up about the nuthouse already!"

Jeff backed into a corner of the seat.

Good for him. Then it hit me. I shouldn't have used that nickname for Ginny. Jeff and I, and a few other boys, always called her that, when she was not around. Now, it didn't feel right. I was making fun of another human being. "Hey, Jeff, I shouldn't have said that about Virginia. I'm sorry." It bothered me how calling her a name sort of slipped out of my mouth. I guess it's easy to fall into that kind of thing, even when you know it's wrong. It's like a bad habit.

Jeff dropped back in his seat. "I shouldn't have said that about the nuthouse. I was only joking, but it isn't cool. I'm just so curious about the numbers. Why do you really think your Grandpa has them?"

"I don't know. But if it makes you happy, I'll ask him tonight. But no more bull about the nuthouse. Deal?"

"And no more threats about Virginia, ever?"

"Maybe." I laughed at how scared Jeff had looked. "Deal," I said, and sank back against the hard leather seat. I was exhausted. It was a long and strange day.

Did I get closer to solving the mystery of how my family was murdered? Maybe, a little. One thing changed: I now definitely, absolutely, positively, wanted to know the whole story, no matter how scary. I made up my mind that nothing, not Mom, Dad, crazy Jeff, not even an earthquake or tornado, would stop me from finally learning the truth. Grandpa wanted to tell me and I wanted to know, even if it scared the pants off me. No rotten Hitler could hurt my family and get away with it. He and his bullies had done enough to Grandpa. I was going to solve this mystery once and for all, and get back to my life as it was before all this started.

"Where's Grandpa," I asked the second I saw Mom was home early, sitting by the phone. The look on her face told me there'd be no chocolate today, not even a little half. "Mom, what's wrong?"

Mom walked over, wrapped her arms around me, and said, "I don't know how to tell you this…."

CHAPTER 19

"It's all the stress about that awful building," Dad exclaimed when he got home from the hospital. "He's going to kill himself if he doesn't stop. I've talked and talked until I'm blue in the face, but he's so stubborn."

"Is Grandpa okay?" I couldn't eat, watch T.V., or concentrate on anything, after Mom told me Grandpa was rushed in an ambulance to the hospital. Dad was called from work to get over there fast. Was I right all along? Was Grandpa leaving me? I knew he wanted to join Nana in heaven. He missed her more than I even did. But I didn't want him to go. I was just getting to know him.

Dad shook his head. "Your Grandpa is the stubbornest old man on this planet. I swear he's going to kill himself, and me, before this is all over."

"Rob, is Sam okay?" Mom asked. Her eye makeup trailed down her cheek. She tried to wipe it off, but I spotted it.

"It's all this aggravation from when Nana died, moving back here, and now, this nonsense about getting back his house and dragging us all to Poland. It's too much for him. It's too much for me." Dad slumped onto a kitchen chair. "David, please go and put on a clean shirt and pants. Grandpa wants us to visit him at the hospital."

"Do you think that's a good idea?" Mom asked.

Dad gave her a hug. "I think it's time we let our David grow up a little. Don't you?"

"I'll be fine, Mom," I said, even though I don't like hospitals. I had to see Grandpa was okay with my own eyes.

Mom looked at me like I was the one 'leaving.' I don't think she liked that I was growing up. "I'll grab my coat," she said. "But Robert, David hasn't eaten. This is going to cost you. Pizza, afterwards?"

"Deal," Dad said and smiled. "Chris, you drive a hard bargain."

I like restaurant pizza, not school cardboard pizza, but I don't like hospitals. They have a funny smell. I smelled it once when Nana was visiting and got sick with asthma. She could hardly talk. She sounded like someone was squeezing her chest so she couldn't breathe right. The smell tonight reminded me that she didn't come home the last time she was in a hospital, in Florida. I was sorry I didn't get to say good-bye. That couldn't happen with Grandpa.

I didn't share my fear of the hospital with my parents. I held it in as I followed them through the hallways. It was noisy, buzzers ringing, voices calling doctors here, there, and everywhere. There were the sound of wheels rolling on the tiles, coming from all directions. A detective isn't afraid, I reminded myself, but I was glad to feel Dad's hand on my shoulder as we approached an old lady in a faded night dress, leaning on the wall. Her hair was white and all over the place. She looked lost.

"Hi. Do you need help?" Dad asked.

Why did he talk to her? She looked scary, mental.

"Thank you, son, I'm fine," the lady replied in a creaky voice, "You're very kind."

I felt ashamed I was afraid of her. Why can't I be more like Dad? I watched the lady move on, her hand wrapped around the rail on the wall. Dad always tries to help people, even strangers. He's like Mr. Hernandez. Maybe I can introduce him to my new friend someday. And yeah, I decided Mr. H. was a friend, now that I knew him. I still wasn't sure about Principal Robinson and his paddle. I'd have to try harder to be like Dad, I decided.

"Grandpa's in here," Dad whispered. "Let me see if he's awake."

I waited nervously in the hall. There was that funky smell. It was like Mom's cleaning junk...ammonia... vinegar? "Dead rats," I could hear Jeff say. He would know. His father is an exterminator.

"Why is it so cold?" I asked Mom, wishing I had a heavier jacket. My old one was small on me already.

"To stop germs from growing," Mom replied, eyes aimed at the door.

Dad signaled for us. "He's dying to see you both."

I wished he didn't use that word. I was afraid to see Grandpa in the hospital. I held back at the door. All the noise and smells upset me.

"Your Grandpa is going to be fine, David," Dad said. "Don't you want to see for yourself?"

I'm not James Bond. I'm not even as brave as Nancy Drew. I'm just a ten-year-old kid who loves his family. I peered into the room hoping I didn't cry if Grandpa looked bad. Was that Grandpa in the bed? He looked too tiny. Maybe it was a large bed? That can make someone look smaller than they really are.

Squealing wheels startled me. A man was on a gurney, staring up at the ceiling. I followed Mom into the room.

When Grandpa saw me, a weak smile appeared on his face. His hair looked as if it had been in a wind storm, like the old lady in the hall. Hospital hair? "I am so happy to see you," he said, reaching his hand toward me. "Come closer, my children."

I was afraid to touch Grandpa's hand. His arm had all these wires and tubes sticking out of it. His skin looked black and blue, as if he fell off a bicycle, or was in a huge fight...and lost. His voice sounded creaky, like the old lady. "Are you okay, Grandpa?" I wanted to hug him, but was afraid I might break him.

"How are you, Sam?" Mom leaned so close I could smell her perfume, much nicer than the hospital smell.

"Dear children, I am good. Come closer. I only need the sunshine from your sweet faces." Grandpa smiled, but looked very tired, as if he couldn't keep his eyes open. "So tell me, Duvidel, what is the best thing what happened to you today?"

"Grandpa, you'll be proud of me," I said, excited to share my news, thinking it would make him happy. "I did a lot of detective work all by myself. I know about Hitler and—"

"Not now David," Dad cut in. "Let Grandpa rest. When he comes home, you can tell him all about it. Okay son?" He pulled me gently aside. "Grandpa is weak. He needs his rest."

My face must have shown my disappointment because Grandpa said softly, "So, now, my brilliant grandson, you know everything what there is to know?"

I never should have said anything. He really sounded weak. I shook my head. "No. Just some stuff. I wanted you to tell me the rest…tonight."

Mom took my hand. "This is not the time, Sweetheart. I promise when we get home, Dad and I will tell you everything you need to know." She smiled at Grandpa and he closed his eyes.

I didn't want Grandpa to get any sicker because of me. I was sorry I said anything. I was selfish. "Sorry, Grandpa."

"Help me sit up a little," Grandpa said. "Come, son, help your old father sit up?"

"Papa, you should rest," Dad replied, "We don't want you to have another attack. I'll tell David everything later. I promise."

"Please, Sam?" Mom said, her face showing such tenderness that I was really worried about Grandpa. "You should rest now." She dropped her palm on his hand. "Dad, we love you and want you to get better fast."

I saw tears in Grandpa's eyes, and then, he closed them again.

I stared at Grandpa, feeling awful he had a heart attack. I was really afraid that like Grandma, he wasn't going to come home from the hospital. *Oh God, not again!* "You have to come home," I said, not thinking about how much trouble I was going to be in for upsetting him. "If you don't come home, we'll never get to Poland."

Grandpa's eyes opened, and his voice sounded a hair stronger. "Don't you worry, my Duvidel, your Grandpa is a stubborn old man. There is no way we are not going to Poland." He gave me a weak smile and closed his eyes.

I wondered if being stubborn could make a person get well, even from a heart attack. When I looked at Dad, he was smiling. Even better, he was holding Grandpa's hand.

CHAPTER 20

Grandpa remained in the hospital for four weeks. He then went to something called rehab for five more. We visited him sometimes after school, but it was hard to talk with everybody around. He complained about the doctors and nurses, and all the exercises he had to do to make his heart stronger. "They always want me to be like a slave. Do this exercise. Do that. Don't they know I'm an old man?"

"Dad, that is what rehab is for. The exercises help your heart get strong," Mom said.

Grandpa shook his head. "You, and Duvidel, my lovely grandson, are the best medicine. And the food? It is terrible! Who can get well eating such garbage? What kind of hospital doesn't know how to make matzoh ball soup?"

Mom said as long as he was complaining, Grandpa was getting better.

Helping Grandpa get better was more important than solving the mystery of what happened to our family fifty years before I was born. Seeing Grandpa close to 'leaving' me, I didn't risk upsetting him again. Mom and Dad were right all along. Maybe I was too young to learn of the Holocaust horrors. Anyway, I didn't ask my parents more questions because they were busy with Grandpa getting better. So was I.

That doesn't mean I completely gave up on solving the mystery. If Grandpa couldn't help me, I decided to try again on my own. But how? I wanted to apologize to Mrs. Goldstein, especially if she might become my teacher in sixth grade. I didn't want her to remember me as a bad kid, just in case I landed in her class. It would be my rotten luck.

71

After stalling a couple of days to build up courage, I decided to talk to Mrs. Goldstein, on a Friday, after lunch. I won't lie, I was very nervous. I almost turned back when I saw her at her desk with a large pile of papers. Jeff said she was mean, but I forced myself to knock on her door. Really softly. I kind of hoped she wouldn't hear me.

Mrs. Goldstein looked up. She had a curious expression on her face, but got off her chair. When she opened the door she looked at me for a long minute. "Weren't you the boy at lunch the other day?"

"I came to apologize." I blurted, stood still, afraid of Mrs. Goldstein yelling at me. She didn't last time. Most likely she was too busy with the crazy kids in the lunch room.

Mrs. Goldstein smiled. "Mr. Robinson told me about his meeting with you. He said you're a very good kid and you didn't mean to do anything wrong."

Was she apologizing to me? "Thank you. I'm sorry. I didn't mean to upset you."

"Would you like to come in?" Mrs. Goldstein held the door open.

I had to squeeze past her. Mrs. Goldstein was a big woman. Jeff said she looked like a walrus. I laughed when he said that. Now, I didn't think it was funny, but I agreed with him that we didn't want her as our sixth grade teacher. But that was when I was judging 'books by their covers.' "Thank you," I said, nervous about being in her room.

I was never in Mrs. Goldstein's room before. I was surprised at how great it looked. She had bulletin boards full of photos of rockets and airplanes. She had lots of student papers, most with gold stars on top. In the back of her room, she had cool-looking projects on shelves. I spotted a pyramid, a bunch of great-looking mummies, and racks of other fun things her students made. "Your room is cool," I said. "I really mean it."

"Thank you. I like doing projects with my students. Do you like making things?"

"I like solving mysteries."

"Well, some of my students do that too." Mrs. Goldstein returned to her chair. "I understand from Principal Robinson that you are working on a mystery now. That is why you had the swastika?"

Trouble coming. "I was stupid. I didn't mean to hurt anyone."

Mrs. Goldstein smiled. "I believe you." She twisted her hair like Mom does, but her hair was gray. "I shouldn't let things like that get to me. It brings back terrible memories. Do you understand?"

I nodded. "My Grandpa too. He lost his whole family during the Holocaust."

"Mr. Robinson told me," Mrs. Goldstein said. "He explained that you didn't know about the swastika."

"I didn't until...recently," I replied, not wanting to get Mr. Hernandez in trouble. When Mrs. Goldstein was in her chair and smiling, she didn't look that scary. Her dress had pretty colored flowers on it. Mom liked flowers. "May I ask you something? Please, don't get upset again."

Mrs. Goldstein nodded.

I took a deep breath. "Can you tell me how my Grandfather's parents and his brothers and sisters died?"

Mrs. Goldstein looked surprised. "You mean during the Holocaust?"

"Yes. Grandpa was telling me but he had a heart attack. I don't want to make him sick again, so I thought I can find out for myself. I want to make him proud of me."

"I see. Don't you think you should ask your parents?"

"I would. Mom isn't Jewish, so I don't think she knows much, and Dad comes home late. He visits Grandpa in the hospital. I thought, maybe, you could help me."

Mrs. Goldstein's eyes looked sad. "David, I would love to help you, but I don't even know how my grandparents died."

"I don't understand. How can so many people be killed by one man and nobody knows what happened to them?"

"It is scary. Isn't it?" Mrs. Goldstein pulled out a small black book from her desk. "This is the only picture I have of my mother as a little girl. Would you like to see?"

The photo was torn and faded. The girl in the snapshot wore a white dress and had a large bow in her dark hair. She was seated on a wood chair, her leather shoes, topped by white socks that ended below her knees, couldn't reach the floor. What surprised me most was the little girl had the most

73

serious face I'd ever seen on a small kid. "How old was she?" I asked, unable to break away from the sad little face in the black and white photograph.

"She was four. This was taken a few days before my grandparents gave her away."

"They gave her away? Why did they do that?" My parents could never give me away, not even if I got in real trouble.

Mrs. Goldstein looked hard at the picture. "My grandparents knew the only chance for her to live was to send her away. They gave her to a family in England. A small number of Jewish children were saved that way." She closed the book. "They never saw their parents again. I...I don't know what happened to my grandparents."

Was Mrs. Goldstein going to cry? "I'm sorry. I shouldn't have asked you."

"I wish I could help you more. We tried finding out what happened to my Grandparents, but never could. Mom was adopted by an English Christian family that raised her as their own. They were very good to her. After a few years, she forgot about her parents and being Jewish."

"I'm half Jewish," I said. "Mom isn't Jewish. Dad is...sort of. He doesn't believe in anything anymore...not even God."

Mrs. Goldstein smiled. "I'm sure he still believes in something."

"I don't think so. Grandpa and Dad fight all the time about that. I hate when they do that."

"I know how that is." Mrs. Goldstein sighed and looked at her papers. "David, I really think you should talk to your parents about what is troubling you. They'll want to help. They love you."

I got up. "Do you teach about the Holocaust in sixth grade?" I asked, thinking I might have to wait only a few more months to learn about it.

Mrs. Goldstein laughed, but got serious quickly. "It's not really funny. In sixth grade we teach world history. I love learning about other cultures. I think you will too." She picked up a thick history book. "The thing is, we start with prehistoric people, then Egypt and the Middle East. We're supposed to get all the way up to today." She flipped open the book. We almost never do. This book has 500 pages."

"Do we have to know all that?" I could never remember everything in such a thick book. I'm not Einstein.

"No, that's impossible. What I'm saying is that because we have so much to learn about we have very little time to get to recent history, if we start from the beginning."

I looked at the mummies in the back of the room. "I'd like to make mummies," I said.

"So do I. I also like studying about African civilizations, India, and China. The kids love it too. But we have almost no time left to learn about World War 2 and the Holocaust before the year ends."

"Are you kidding? It changed everybody's lives and nobody teaches about it?"

"I didn't say that. We teach about it, but near the end of the year. David, you know I'd love to spend more time helping kids understand what happened, especially because it was so close to me. But with everything we have to learn before our state tests in May, we can't do it."

"Mom says there's no such word as can't." I forgot how afraid I was of Mrs. Goldstein or I would never have said that.

"I agree with your mother. But I'm not the one who decides what goes into the text books or what we teach. We do a Holocaust story in our reading book about Anne Frank. Do you know about her?"

I shook my head.

"She was a Jewish teenager who kept a diary while hiding from the Nazis in an attic."

"Can she tell me how my family died?" I wondered if anyone could help me solve this mystery.

Mrs. Goldstein looked uneasy. "David, Anne Frank died during the war."

Another one dead? "The girl died...or was she murdered? Grandpa says my whole family was murdered—"

"David, I really have to pick up my class." Mrs. Goldstein stood.

"Mrs. Goldstein, please tell me? Was she murdered too?"

Mrs. Goldstein looked undecided and then said, "Anne Frank was captured by the Nazis and—"

"How did she die?" That's what I wanted to know.

Mrs. Goldstein shook her head. "David, you are a wonderful boy. Your parents, your grandfather should be proud of you. I see you care." She placed a hand on my shoulder. "Anne Frank died from disease and hunger in a concentration camp. She was only a teen-ager. It's sad. Imagine what she might have been if she were allowed to grow up? Imagine what they all could have been?"

I was no longer afraid of Mrs. Goldstein. She was trying her best to help me. "Thank you, Mrs. Goldstein. I'm sorry she died like that." I gulped, a lump in my throat. "Do you think that's how my family died too?"

"I am going to be honest with you, David. I can't wait until you are in my class. You and I will explore many mysteries together, but I can't tell you anymore now. You really need to talk to your parents. I have to go and get my class."

"I understand. Thank you, Mrs. Goldstein." I prepared to leave, still without the answers I wanted.

"David, may I tell you something?"

I nodded, a little afraid of what she was going to say.

"The Holocaust is one of the hardest things to teach about. Even for me. There are things that happened, things that were done, that are hard to believe, impossible to understand. Some things were so horrible we can't mention them in school. But, I think you are right. We do need to teach it more. Thank you, David."

I smiled. "May I ask you one last question?"

She nodded. "Please, make it fast."

"What does 'systematic extermination' mean?"

Mrs. Goldstein turned white as a ghost. "I'm sorry, David, I really have to go now."

"Thank you, Mrs. Goldstein. I really appreciate your help."

Mrs. Goldstein closed her door, locked it, and said, "David, I'm sorry I couldn't help more. You need to talk to your parents before you learn something you can't handle. I meant what I said. I can't wait until you're up here next year. You're quite a boy."

I walked to my math class thinking about how was I going to tell Jeff I wanted Mrs. Goldstein for my sixth grade teacher. He'd never go for it.

CHAPTER 21

A fter my talk with Mrs. Goldstein, I wasn't sure what to do about my mystery. I thought about going back to her a few days later and see if I could dig out more information. That's what a real detective would do. But if I pushed too hard, she might decide to call my parents. With Grandpa in the hospital, I didn't want to give them another problem. Like Mom says, "If you're not part of the solution, then you're part of the problem." I decided to let things slide for a while. After my last disasters, I thought I should be a little more careful where I poked my nose.

I did go to the library and borrow the book by Anne Frank. I read it at home while Mom was working. At first, I thought it was just a diary of a girl. I usually don't read books about girls, so I almost put it down. It wasn't going to tell me what I really wanted to know: how my family was killed. As I read more, I began to understand, not only what Anne experienced, but what my family suffered. I was sad, reading how her family had to hide in a tiny attic with a bunch of strangers. They couldn't make any noise. Walking, going outside, doing any of the things I took for granted, were forbidden or they might be detected. I would have hated hiding, cooped up with only grown-ups, worried all the time that you might be found and killed.

Anne's book almost lost me again when she started writing about liking boys and all that 'mushy' stuff. Then I realized that dying so young, many of the Holocaust victims, including Grandpa's brothers and sisters, missed out on so much. They never had the chances I had. They never went to college, explored their interests, found a career. They would never fall in love, get married, have children. It made me see Anne and that kiss differently. I would have lost out on so much if I was born at that time…if I was Anne Frank or Grandpa, or my sweet Nana. The more I learned about the Holocaust, the more I realized how lucky I was.

Anne Frank's diary made the suffering of my Grandfather, and all children from that terrible time, come to life for me. It was her own words, her private feelings, her hopes and dreams. They were the last words of a girl who might have been in my school, my class, my friend. From what happened to her, I began to understand the terrible human cost of Hitler's hate of Jews. It made me angry and sad because my Grandpa and Nana suffered too. I didn't know how anyone could make others suffer so much. Did they enjoy hurting others? Didn't they have a conscience? What was wrong with them? Did God make them with something missing? When Anne wrote that she still believed most people are good, I put the book down. How could she believe that after everything she went through? Did I believe that after what I was learning?

One afternoon, a few weeks later, I came home from school expecting an empty house, as usual. Imagine my surprise. Grandpa was sitting in Dad's favorite chair. He was dressed in his old blue robe and brown slippers, looking as if he'd been there all along. The T.V. was blasting. (He says he has cotton plants growing in his ears, but the truth is his hearing is not very good.)

"You're home?" I wasn't sure he was real. "Are you okay? Is your heart okay? Do you have to go back? Can I get you anything? You're really home?"

Grandpa laughed and lowered the T.V. sound. "Slow down, Duvidel. I can't answer so many questions. The important one: Yes, I'm home for good. Thank God. The food there was terrible. I could kill for matzoh ball soup."

"That's cool, Grandpa." I looked him over as if I never saw him before. It was if I was checking to see if all of my Grandpa was here, or if he was like a mirage…or a ghost.

Grandpa waved the remote. "So, you don't mind my taking over your living room a few weeks? The doctors won't let me go to my place. They're a pain in the neck. They want I should stay here. Is it okay with you?"

"Are you kidding?" I rushed to give Grandpa a big hug, but was afraid I would hurt him. He looked even weaker than before. I could see bones right through his skin, which was very white. I could see veins and black and blue marks on the top of his hands.

"I won't break," Grandpa said, as if reading my mind, and he reached for me.

There were blue numbers on his arm.

It all came rushing back.

Grandpa must have seen the strange look on my face. He said, "So David, tell your old Grandpa -and yes, now I am old at last- what is wrong? Why do you look so strange on me?"

I was too curious. I should have kept my big mouth shut. "Grandpa, my best friend, Jeff, wants to know...I want to know... why do you have those blue numbers on your arm?" I was sorry I asked. He needed rest and I bugged him about a dumb tattoo.

Grandpa stared at his arm as if he never noticed the numbers before. "It is a good question," he said slowly. "I never told you this?"

Grandpa liked my question? "My friend, Jeffrey — he's crazy— says it's because you were once in prison." I didn't want to tell him that Jeff also said he was in a nuthouse. As if prison was any better. "I'm sorry, Grandpa, I shouldn't ask now." What was wrong with me? He was getting over a heart attack. Did I want him to have another one because of me? "Let's forget about it and watch T.V."

Grandpa looked puzzled. "I could swear I told you this. I am getting old and forgetful. So, I'm glad you ask." He straightened himself up in his...in Dad's chair. "Your friend is right. I was in prison, a terrible prison."

"You committed a crime?" I didn't want to know any more.

Grandpa sighed and I heard a wheeze as if he swallowed a tiny whistle. Nana sounded that way too. "If being Jewish is a crime," he said softly, "then, yes, I committed a crime."

"I don't understand." I was glad Dad came back from the bathroom just then.

"You don't understand what, David?" Dad asked. "How are you doing, Papa?"

"Duvidel wants to know about my numbers." Grandpa raised his arm a little off the armrest.

"Oh, David, he just got here. Give him a rest. Don't you have homework?"

"Jeff thought Grandpa was a criminal because of the numbers on his arm," I said, knowing it was wrong to blame Jeff. No detective on T.V. would do such a cowardly thing.

Mom was listening from the kitchen doorway. "David, you know your Grandpa could never do anything illegal."

"I know," I said, embarrassed. "But Jeff said. Oh heck! Sorry Grandpa. I told him he was nuts."

"You tell your friend that Grandpa could never hurt anyone," Mom said and smiled at Grandpa.

"Thank you, Christine." Grandpa gave her a weak smile.

"Then why was he in prison? That's what Grandpa just said." Why didn't I just drop it? It was an unsolved mystery. A detective can't have peace when a mystery isn't solved.

Grandpa looked at Dad. "Duvidel should know."

Dad nodded. "But take it easy, Papa. You're not supposed to get excited."

Grandpa sighed again. "They baby me. I told you, Duvidel, I am growing backwards." He folded his hands in his lap. "You see, Boychick," (That means, 'little boy', which is what he called my Dad sometimes, when they weren't fighting.) "I am calm." He turned toward me. "You remember when I tell you about the Nazi soldiers? How they are coming to our house and taking everybody away on big trucks."

I didn't want to tell him I had nightmares about those awful soldiers breaking down doors and everybody screaming. I didn't have those dreams for a while. Did I want to have them again? Was it too late to stop him?

"I never have a chance to finish the story. You know why." Grandpa sounded tired.

"You don't have to tell me now," I said. "You're tired."

Grandpa shook his head. "I owe you this. I owe this to my parents, also my brothers and sisters. Your sweet Nana, may she rest in peace; she would want me to finish too."

Dad draped his arm around my shoulder.

That should have made me feel protected. Instead, I was afraid of what I was about to learn.

CHAPTER 22

It was hard to look at Grandpa's face, creased with painful memories. His hands, bonier than ever, shook, as he spoke. "So, I left off with the trucks, I think. I told you of the soldiers with big rifles. They was keeping us back, as one-by-one, so many were taken away in the night. We didn't know where. They was gone forever." He gazed at me as he caught his breath. "It is hard for you to understand, living here, free, in America. Imagine, David, how you would feel if one day all your family and friends was taken away, and you can never find out what happens to them? You can search all your life for those you love. But there is no hope of finding what happened. Can you imagine such a thing?"

"That's awful." I was glad Dad was with me. This was getting scary again.

"Yes, it was awful. One night, we was sleeping in the house. I heard running up the stairs. It was the soldiers. I thought they was coming for somebody else. We did nothing to them."

"Hitler's soldiers?"

Grandpa nodded. "This time, they smash down our door. One hits my father in the face with his fist. For no reason. They scream at us, "Get out! Get out! Dirty Jews! Get out!"

I can hear them screaming. "Get out! Dirty Jews! Get out!" I want to hide behind Dad.

Grandpa continues, "I was so frightened I was not thinking straight. My father was on the floor. Like he was shot. I didn't know if he was dead or alive. It happens so fast."

"Did they kill him?" I had icicles on my skin. I heard Tony scream, "Dirty

83

Jew! Drop dead, you dirty Jew!" How can anyone say "drop dead" to someone? How would they feel if it came true? Maybe bullies like Tony and Hitler don't care. Maybe they're not human. No. They are human. That's the scariest thing I learned. The haters and murderers are human.

Mom was seated with us. She looked more pale than usual. Her skin is much whiter than ours, like ivory, another clue that she is different than Dad and me. None of her family sound like Russian spies when they talk. I used to make Mom laugh when I imitated her mother's Boston accent.

"Duvidel asked me about my father. No. They did not kill my poor Papa. Not yet." Grandpa looked at the window, as if checking that he was here, with us, and not back in that scary night. Then he spoke again, "We was all rushed down the stairs with only a few things what we could grab in our hands. We could break our necks from all the pushing. The Nazi soldiers are screaming at us, and threatening us with guns, charging us into the street in the front of the building...in the middle of the night."

"Is that the building you want back?" I asked.

"It was our home and the Nazis stole it from us. It was our home!"

"Papa, calm down. Your heart. You can't get excited. Please Papa?" Dad reached for his father's hand.

"Sam, please take it easy?" Mom gave Grandpa a worried look.

I was worried about him too. "Grandpa, you can stop. I can wait until you're better."

Grandpa was breathing hard. "I want to go on. I will be calm." He waited a few seconds before beginning again. "I will stay calm. The soldiers force us into trucks. They beat or shoot anyone who does not obey. I saw this myself."

"But that's against the law," I interrupted, glad that could never happen in the USA.

"David," Dad said, "You don't understand. Hitler was a dictator. That means he controlled everything. He made up all the laws. Nobody, not the people in Germany, Poland, or even the United States were able to stop him."

"He was stronger than the President?" I found that hard to believe.

Grandpa grunted. "It was incredible. Millions of innocent people was taken from their homes and forced to be slaves because Hitler wanted it."

"You were a slave?" Principal Robinson said his family were slaves too. Maybe that's why he wanted to know what happened to my family.

Grandpa shifted in his seat. "Yes. The lucky ones was slaves."

"Sam, don't frighten him anymore. Please?" Mom looked at Grandpa with pleading eyes.

Grandpa nodded. "David, they took us from the trucks to a long line of trains. We was told we are being moved to a safe place away from the war. We are loaded into cattle cars, eighty, maybe a hundred of us, maybe more, in a car what moves cows. We have to stand, crowded, stinky...three or four days, we stand—"

"There were no seats?" I got tired just standing on line for lunch on pizza Fridays. It goes all the way down the hall. How could anyone stand on a moving train for days?

"No seats and no toilets. Just two buckets. One for dirty water for drinking. The other for... for..." He looked puzzled.

"Pooping and peeing," Dad said.

"Oh! No toilets? That's gross!"

"Yes, Duvidel, it was gross. The stink was everywhere. But the worse was we was so cold, hungry and tired. People was dropping all around us...sick... dead...in filth."

Mom shot Dad a look, squeezing his hand.

Dad immediately said, "Papa, you're tired. We'll finish tomorrow."

Not again! Wasn't I ever going to learn the whole story? "What about the numbers? Please, Grandpa, I need to know about the numbers... to tell Jeff. So he stops bugging me."

Grandpa closed his eyes. Was he trying to remember something? "When we got to the end of the long train trip, those still alive, was told to stand on a long line—"

"Papa, no more. Please? David really will have nightmares," Dad said.

I never saw Dad so edgy. "But what about the numbers?" I asked again. "Just tell me about them?"

Grandpa sighed. "Your papa is right. I am tired, but I will tell you what you want...what your friend, Jeffrey, wants to know. Okay?" He looked at Dad.

"But this is the end for tonight," Dad said. "Absolutely, no more."

Grandpa nodded. "The numbers...these numbers was tattooed on my arm by the Nazis, so I could not escape. We was branded like animals, so all would know we are slaves...no more human."

The picture I saw in my brain, my Grandpa forced to have numbers tattooed into his flesh, like an animal, made me angrier than anything else so far. At that moment, the blue letters on his arm, Grandpa branded like a horse or cow, was the most disgusting thing I ever heard.

"Did it hurt?" I stared at his arm, covered by the blue sleeve of his robe, and saw the numbers, even though they were hidden by the furry fabric. It was as if I had x-ray vision and was seeing the horror burnt forever into his flesh. Now, I understood they were the mark of slavery. I hated those ugly numbers and the people who had used needles to tattoo them into my Grandpa's skin. I hated those numbers so much that my stomach hurt. It wasn't fair. How could anyone hurt my Grandpa like that? I pictured him being held down and...I didn't want to see it. I never felt so angry, so awful. My head hurt. My stomach was twisting worse with each second.

Something else bothered me, but it was difficult to put into words. I couldn't figure out why I was so angry, so disgusted, about one tattoo on my Grandpa's arm and didn't feel that way when I heard that six million Jews, and six million other people, were killed by Hitler and his murderers. What was wrong with me? How could I hear about the death of millions of men, women and children, and be less upset than when I heard what the Nazis did to Grandpa's arm?

The more I learned about the Holocaust, the more confused I was. I couldn't understand how anyone could do such horrible things. I didn't understand the feelings inside me as I stared at my Grandfather's arm and those awful numbers.

"Yes, Duvidel, the numbers hurt," Grandpa replied. "But it was not the worst."

I felt sick. I wanted to stop, but I had one more question. "Did Nana have numbers too?"

Mom's voice was very soft when she replied, "David, yes."

CHAPTER 23

A detective searches for all the clues to a crime. It can be a fingerprint, a phone message, or a few seconds where a killer's alibi isn't enough to hide a murder. One tiny detail, one piece of the puzzle, can be the clue that stays in your brain until you find the solution to your case. Sometimes that detail can be like a sorcerer's curse, not letting you think of anything else. It was strange how the details of Grandpa's story haunted me. They bothered me more than everything that happened to millions of human beings.

I kept thinking about not having toilets on the cattle cars. It was stuck in my mind as if that was the most horrible part of hundreds of people, men, women, and children being crowded together into railroad cars for days. I felt as if I was going to throw-up from the imagined stink. It was a tiny detail in a true-life horror story. No toilets.

Another image I couldn't shake was the picture of my Grandpa, and Nana, who never hurt anyone, held down by black gloved hands of faceless soldiers while numbers were branded into their flesh. I imagined Grandpa not giving the 'monsters' the satisfaction of hearing him scream. He would shut his eyes and bear the pain in clenched silence. In my nightmares, I heard Nana's screams.

I was angry and confused. I felt sad, sadder than ever before. The truth is my life was happy until I learned about our past. Now, I couldn't forget it and couldn't ignore it. Mom was right, it was scary, horrible, and made me sick. I didn't want to feel this way. I knew I should talk to my parents, but they would think I was a baby. Besides, Grandpa had been living with us for weeks, and as Dad says, he was a 'handful.' Talk to Jeff? I answered my own question. So, who could I trust? Who could help me understand what I felt raging inside me?

Mr. Hernandez was in his office at the rear of the school basement when I got up the nerve to go see him. "Buenos dias, Amigo," he said with a large smile when I peeked into his room. "I am very glad to see you. It has been a while."

I sat on the gray chair opposite Mr. Hernandez' cluttered desk. It was a swivel chair, so I turned around in circles. Should I trust him? I really didn't know him well. Was this a mistake? I made quite a few lately. Remember the paddle?

"So how are you, David?" Mr. Hernandez reached inside his desk.

I stopped the chair. "I'm okay." What was he digging out of the drawer?

"I hoped for you to tell me what you learned." Mr. Hernandez offered me a chocolate bar, which I took, since it was wrapped. Mom always says, "Never eat unwrapped candy. It could be poisoned." I never believed anyone would do something so evil. Now, after all I learned, I believed people were capable of all kinds of terrible things.

"David, are you hokay?"

"Yeah." I took a second to enjoy the chocolate. "I think I've figured out most of my mystery, Mr. Hernandez, but there are still pieces missing."

"There always are in something so big. So, how can I help you, mi amigo?"

Him saying that, and the chocolate, made me feel a little more relaxed. "My Grandpa told me why he has numbers on his arm. Do you know about that?"

"Si. I know." He looked disgusted. "It was like how they branded slaves in this country. Terrible. Hard to believe it happened here too. They do to human beings like they do to horses and cows. I am sorry you learn of this thing."

I forgot they branded slaves in America. I believed that it could never happen here. I was ashamed to ask my next question. He would think I was a bad person.

"So what is your question? Don't be afraid to ask." Mr. Hernandez offered me another candy.

"No, thank you." I handed him my wrapper. "Mr. Hernandez, I don't understand something."

"Only one thing? I don't understand many things." He chuckled.

I felt I could trust him. "Mr. Hernandez, please don't think I'm a bad person?"

He looked surprised. "I could never think of my friend as bad. What is bothering you so?"

It was time to tell someone. "I don't understand something. I got really, really, mad when Grandpa told me about the tattoos on his and Nana's arms. I hate the Germans who did that. I really hate them." I didn't see a reaction on his face, so I continued. "I never hated anyone before." I appreciated his listening to me, not talking, just listening, so I went on. "What I don't understand is why that 'tattoo' made me so angry? I feel like I could kill whoever did that to my Grandpa and Nana."

Mr. Hernandez was still silent.

I continued, hoping he didn't think I was a bad person for what I was about to say. "When I heard millions of people were killed by Hitler, I didn't get mad. I didn't cry, or anything. Don't I care?" I felt ashamed telling him, but it bothered me a lot. "The truth is, and I don't like admitting it, I didn't feel anything. Is there something wrong with me?"

Mr. Hernandez looked thoughtful. "David, I wonder about this many times. It is hard to understand how people feel so terrible when a pet dies but feel nothing when they see on television so many people dead in a war, earthquake, or something else. Is this what you mean?"

"I think so. How come I don't feel anything about millions of people being killed? How can others not care? Are we like Hitler?" *Is that why I didn't help the bullied kid? I should have at least tried. I might have stopped the bully.*

Mr. Hernandez shook his head. "No, David. Never like Hitler." He paused. "Maybe it is too hard to believe so many people could be killed like this. Si? I think it is easier to feel pain when a person close to you is hurt."

"That makes sense. That is why I feel so bad about Nana and Grandpa."

"Yes. Hearing millions died is difficult to think is real. So, you don't cry like you do for your Grandpa's tattooed arm. It is real for you. And you love him. Si?"

I nodded. I did love him, now that I knew him better.

Mr. Hernandez sighed. "Millions being killed is hard to believe, even for me. It is impossible to see as real number. Who can imagine such a thing? Is this making sense?"

"I guess." I thought back to how I cried when my friend Julie's dog was hit by a car. It was like the most horrible thing that ever happened. Just seeing Julie later made me feel like crying. "So if I know someone—"

"David, think how you would feel if someone hurts your Mama or Papa? God forbid. Would this not make you angry, more angry, than hearing thousands of children are starving in some far off place, like Africa, or even in America? We have many starving children here, in the United States, but unless it hurts someone you know—"

"I'd kill anyone who hurt my parents." My stomach was churning. "So, I'm not an evil person because I don't cry for all those poor men, women and children who were killed by Hitler?"

"No, David, I know you are a very good person. You care much. You want to know the truth, even if it frightens you. This makes you a good person, someone I am proud to call, mi amigo."

"Thank you, Mr. Hernandez. You're a big help." I wasn't sure I understood completely, but he made me feel I wasn't the only one who found it impossible to believe what happened. It did seem unreal, a long distance and time away.

"I am glad I help you. Any other questions?" Mr. Hernandez held up the dish of candy. "More chocolate, mi amigo?"

"No thank you." I hesitated before asking one more question that had also been bothering me. "Mr. Hernandez, is it always wrong to hate someone? That's what Mom and Dad taught me."

"Si. I think so. Hitler, he was full of hate, what made him muy vicious." He touched the large silver cross dangling on a thin chain under his shirt. "Jesus tells how wrong it is to hate other people, any people. You understand? All religions teach hate is wrong. So yes, it is wrong."

"My Grandfather hates all Germans and Polish people for what they did to our family. Is that wrong?" I didn't tell him I now felt that way too. I was afraid he would be ashamed of me.

"This is a tough question. Your Grandpapa, he has good reasons to curse the people who did such horrible things to his family. It is difficult to forgive such things. No?"

"Yes. But Dad says it was a long time ago, and Grandpa should get over it."

Mr. Hernandez smiled. "Your father sounds like a good man. He is right, but I think it is hard to forgive something so terrible."

"I think so too."

Mr. Hernandez' eyes looked kind. "I am sorry, David, mi amigo. For you this must be very hard to learn. Imagine you are your Grandpapa. Can you forgive this if you were him?"

I couldn't even forgive the Nazis for what they did to Grandpa's arm. "So, Grandpa is right to want revenge?"

Mr. Hernandez looked at me for a long time and said, "You are asking very hard questions today. I don't know what to answer." He rubbed his forehead. "I don't know if I can forgive if someone hurt my Elena or my two sons?" He looked at the photograph on his desk. "Your Grandpapa, he lose much…but those who did these terrible things are dead, or so old, they must soon face God. God will judge them. Yes, I think that is the answer."

I didn't tell him Dad didn't believe in God anymore, and I wasn't sure what I thought. After all, how could God let such terrible things happen? "So, you're saying we should let them get away with what they did?"

"More tough questions. I believe God will judge them. But David, my friend, just like it is wrong to hate all Jews, I think it is wrong to blame all Germans and Polish people too. I do not think all Germans and Polish were bad people even then. Si? And the children, and grandchildren, did not do these terrible things. Is it fair to blame them too?"

"I don't know. That's why I'm asking you."

"I wish I have a simple answer. You must talk to your parents."

"I will, but Mr. Hernandez, what's bothering me is…I hate the Germans and Poles now." Was he disappointed in me? "I don't want to hate anyone. It hurts my head and stomach. I was happier when I didn't have this inside me. Do you know what I mean?"

Mr. Hernandez nodded. "Yes. You are right, David. These are awful feelings for everybody. I hated and know how sick I feel too. It is a terrible feeling inside. Si. I know." He stood up. "You are a very bright boy. I think you know the answers already." He walked toward the door. "I have learned something from you today, mi amigo. I too must stop feeling so angry for what was done in the past. Perhaps, you will teach your Grandfather this."

I didn't understand what Mr. Hernandez thought I taught him. I was as confused as ever. In my head, I knew I should not hate anyone, but after all I learned about what happened to my Grandpa, I blamed every German and Pole. Like Grandpa, I wanted to get even. I wanted them to know what it felt like. If someone hurt or murdered, your family, wouldn't you want revenge?

CHAPTER 24

In the weeks that followed, I picked up more details about what happened to my family. Mom was right as usual. Grandpa's story gave me nightmares, so I won't share everything I learned about the inhuman things the Nazis did. You have to solve some mysteries about this terrible time on your own. It is important to ask your parents and teachers about the Holocaust. It may not be easy to get answers. Some people don't want to talk about the unbelievable things that happened. They may want to protect you as my parents tried to do. Some people don't want to believe it actually happened. I don't either, but it did. Some might not want the painful job of telling about this horrible event in human history. I understand, but hiding your head in the sand doesn't make the danger go away.

Unfortunately, many people forget, or may not know enough about the Holocaust. The last survivors, like my Grandpa, will soon be gone. Their histories will be lost if not recorded. It is important to keep their histories for the future.

I still can't believe how brutal some people can be to others. I understand why Mom and Dad protected me. It really was 'gruesome,' as the computer entry said. It was worse because it was real. Sometimes, I wish I didn't learn so much about the Holocaust. But it is important to understand how something so terrible happened, or like Grandpa says, it could happen again.

Could it happen again? I don't know. Grandpa warned it could, right here in America. I hope not. If everyone remembers it, maybe we can stop something like this from ever happening again to anyone. We'll recognize a 'Hitler' the next time someone spreads messages of hate. I don't like what I learned, but now I know what to look out for. I won't let something like this ever happen again without trying to stop it.

It turns out, I soon faced that test. Tony and two of his friends cornered a fourth grader on the playground. They had the kid surrounded by the handball court wall. I walked past them and then stopped. I turned back and glared at Tony. I thought if he saw someone watching him, he would leave the little kid alone.

"What do you want?" Tony asked. "Get the hell out of here."

A chill raced through me. I looked for the monitor. Nowhere near. "Leave the kid alone," I said.

Tony looked surprised. "Mind your own damn business."

One of his friends made a fist.

I forced myself to keep my hands at my side.

Tony sneered. "You still here?"

"Let him go. He didn't do anything—"

"You're bugging me," Tony said and took a step toward me.

The fourth grader ran off.

Great, I thought, I help him and he gets away. "Tony, you're too big to pick on a little kid like that," I said, hoping he'd listen to reason.

Tony shook his head as if he felt sorry for me. He raised his fist and then dropped it.

I was braced to be clobbered. What stopped him. I looked out of the corner of my eye.

"Hey, Dave," Jeff said, stepping beside me. "You know the others here?"

I looked and saw Virginia, Shante, Rick, and two other friends Jeff and I knew from our School Service club. The cavalry had arrived.

Tony looked at his thugs and then back at Jeff. "You know him?" He asked.

Jeff replied, "He's my best friend."

Tony replied, "You should tell him to mind his own business."

Jeff smiled. "You shouldn't pick on little kids." He walked over to Tony and I realized Jeff was taller and tougher-looking. I never thought of him that way before. "I'll see you at football practice," he said and put his hand on my shoulder.

94

Tony nodded, sneered at me, and then turned away. His two thugs followed. "Thanks Jeff. Thanks guys," I said after I was able to breathe again.

Jeff thanked the others and we walked back to the school doors. He turned to me and said, "You could have got your ass kicked."

"I couldn't see him bully that kid," I replied. "Thanks for saving me."

Jeff took the gum out of his pocket and tossed it into a trash can. "You know, I think you're as crazy as your grandfather...as brave too."

I didn't know if that fourth grader was Jewish or not. And don't get me wrong, I was still afraid of bullies like Tony. But now that I saw how bullying could spread, I hoped I was a little braver. Seeing how the other kids helped me, I realized that was the best way to stop him, or anyone else who wanted to be a bully. If that had happened before World War 2, Hitler might not have been able to do what he did to so many people. Dad says if more of us stuck up for the victims, bullies would back down. I guess that's the most important thing I learned from all this. Without us standing up to stop them, nobody knows who might become the next target.

As Grandpa got better, I was sure that I solved my family's mystery and learned to stand up against bullies. We hardly talked about it anymore. The nightmares stopped and I was excited about going into sixth grade. Mrs. Goldstein turned out to be a great teacher. I did lots of projects about early humans, Egypt, African and Greek/Roman history. It was interesting and a lot of fun. But she was right, by the time we got to the end of the year, we spent only a few minutes on the Holocaust. It didn't matter. I found out what I had to know. I was more interested in girls now, especially Ginny Johnson. Her braces gave her the cutest smile.

After the incident with Tony, Jeff and I were closer than ever. He still drove me nuts but I realized he was someone who cared about me. I was lucky. I had parents, a grandfather, and friends, maybe a girlfriend, who also cared about me. Everything looked great. Nothing prepared me for what came next.

II

POLAND, AUGUST 2001

This is where I'll pick up the final pieces of my terrifying mystery...

Dust makes the apartment building across the street look gray.
Wood boards cover the bottom windows.
"Is this your house, Grandpa?" A detective, even a twelve-year-old, isn't supposed to be afraid, but I know this building's past. This is the land of my family's secret.
"How did we get into this mess?" Dad asks, staring at the building. I wish I knew.

CHAPTER 25

Grandpa moved into our house for good a few months after his heart attack. A year later, he was still here. The doctors said he couldn't live alone anymore. Mom and Dad argued about that in hushed tones, in their bedroom, but I knew. I saw it in their faces. I didn't understand why all the fuss, but soon learned.

Grandpa ended up taking my room. Dad moved all my furniture into our third bedroom, much smaller. He said he would make it up to me someday. I was ticked-off about Grandpa taking my room, but when I saw him fresh from rehab and using a walker, I felt sorry. It wasn't easy being stuck in a small room, and putting up with him blasting the television in the living room, but I said it was fine because I knew Dad was worried about his father. I was too.

It took several weeks, but Grandpa was doing better. The walker was replaced by his four-legged cane and his voice sounded less creaky. He didn't grip my hand anymore, but he looked as if he was stronger. I sometimes came home and caught him on the phone talking in Polish. Somedays, he sounded angry, shouting and raising his fist. When he saw me, he said a few more words and hung up.

I suspected he was being bad, disobeying Dad, stressing himself out about getting back his house. I didn't know why he kept trying. I was afraid it might give him another heart attack.

I told Dad what I suspected.

Dad shrugged and replied, "I know what the stubborn mule is up to.

Reclaiming his house is a lost cause."

After sixty years, I thought so too.

One night, in the kitchen, after Grandpa went into the living room to watch T.V. , Dad held up a bill. He grumbled to Mom that Grandpa's calls to Poland were bankrupting us.

I knew Dad. It wasn't the money that was bothering him. He was worried about his father's health.

"The stress is killing him," Dad continued. "Look at all these phone calls to Poland. He spends hours trying to get back this house and gets nowhere. I wish he'd stop already. Why can't he just enjoy his life with us?"

"It keeps him going," Mom replied.

"It will keep him going right to the cemetery. I wish the Polish government would give in already. He won't. He's too mule-headed."

"Like someone else I know and love."

Mom says that about me too.

"I don't know how much more he can take," Dad said. "I don't know how much I can take." He folded the bill and shoved it in an envelope.

Mom smiled. "Rob, maybe you should help him. It's important to him. It's his dream."

"But it's hopeless, Chris. He's been fighting the Polish government for years. They don't want to give Jews back the property the Nazis took from us."

Mom gave Dad a kiss on the cheek. "Nothing is hopeless once you make up your mind. You're as stubborn as your old man."

"Well, I wish he would give it up already," Dad said. "It was too long ago. Nothing is worth all this."

"Just think about it," Mom said and gave him a kiss on top of his head.

"She always wins," Dad muttered but smiled.

I followed Dad into the living room.

Grandpa was in his robe, watching T.V.. His eyes were so fixed on the set he looked hypnotized.

Dad muted the sound, and out of nowhere, said, "Papa, I love you."

"I love you too," Grandpa replied. "Now turn back on the sound, please?"

Dad held the remote in his hand. "It's because I love you that I want to talk to you."

Grandpa sighed and fell back into the chair.

I sat down on the couch.

Dad glanced at the kitchen door and began, "Papa, isn't it enough you had a heart attack over this house in Poland? It is more than sixty years since the War. Why can't you be satisfied to enjoy the life we have, with the family that loves you?"

"Because I can't," Grandpa said, already sounding annoyed. "Can you? Can you honestly forgive the 'butchers' who wiped out our whole family?"

Dad looked so miserable that I felt sorry for him. "You know I can't. But Papa, the building isn't what's important, and I'm afraid it's killing you."

Grandpa leaned forward and gripped the armrests. "What kills me, my dear son, is why you don't understand what this means to me. What it should mean to all of us."

Oh, oh! Here it comes, another argument. I braced myself for the explosion.

CHAPTER 26

When I was younger, I wondered why my family had so many arguments. Now I had a theory. Grandpa suffered so much at the hands of the Nazis. He lost most of his family in horrible ways. He blamed Nana's sickness, and her leaving us, on German mistreatment during the Holocaust. He didn't think Dad felt the same about our past. I wasn't sure how Dad felt because he didn't usually show his emotions. I was sure he was angry too, but Grandpa and Dad were very different.

One thing I was sure about was that I hated when Grandpa shouted at Dad and the tension after their fights. I imagined how Grandpa became furious when Dad told him he was marrying Mom, a non Jew. That would have been hard to take. The arguing that must have caused…I could almost hear Nana weeping. It was why they moved to Florida. I got it now, but it didn't make it less painful to listen to them during one of their battles.

Grandpa threw the first punch, "You'll never understand. It is a different world for you."

Dad replied, "I do understand, Papa. I hate the Nazis who hurt you. But I love you more. I can't stand to see what this is doing to you."

"You were not there." Grandpa gripped Dad's hands. "I was standing in the line with Mama and Papa, when we arrived at Auschwitz. I had hope we was going to be alright. The officers said they was moving us to a safe place, away from the war. It was a lie. They was moving us closer to the gas chambers—"

"Papa! David is here." Dad shot Grandpa a warning look.

Detective David Jacobs locked onto "gas chambers." What was Grandpa talking about?

Grandpa ignored Dad's warning. "Imagine, Robert, how you would feel if a Nazi ripped your wonderful Duvidel from your arms and you never saw him again? You would fight! As much as you love peace, you would fight. Yes?"

No one's going to take me from my family, I thought, but kept silent.

Grandpa glared at Dad. "Yes, even you, the peace-lover, would fight. But they have rifles, dogs, and black hitting sticks. They would knock you down into the dirt if you dare to speak up. You hear the dogs growling. You could do nothing. Nothing. So, you would never see your sweet David again. And no matter how much you search your whole life, you never know what happens to him." Grandpa's accent was stronger. He looked as if he was about to cry. "This is what happened to me. I lost all of them. All. Can you understand this?"

I didn't want to hear more but couldn't leave.

Grandpa wiped his eyes with his sleeve. "Robert, there is not even one grave. All of them was wiped off the face of the Earth...like they never was."

Dad looked upset. "Papa, I know this. Believe me, I feel what you feel."

"No, you do not, or you would not question why I am fighting so hard. Robert, our house is all what remains. The Germans took it as if we were nothing." Grandpa coughed hard. "The Polish watched as the Nazis tore us to pieces until only a few survive. My whole family...our family was no more. We must take back what is ours, before it is too late...before we are all gone." He stared at my father, and through trembling lips, said, "Who will tell the story when I and all the survivors are gone? It is almost finished. Nobody will remain. Who will remember? Who will tell?"

My father looked at me as if asking if I was allright.

I didn't know. It was horrible. But it was true. The most important thing I understood was the story was not just Grandpa's past, but **my** past. This horrible story was my history. I couldn't walk away from it.

As Grandpa spoke, I saw it all. Thousands of people standing on long lines, men, women and children. Everyone exhausted after getting out of the cramped cattle cars. Grandpa was too weak, frightened, to cry out when without warning the soldiers grabbed my great grandparents. Imagine his horror when other soldiers seized the youngest of his brothers and sisters, and forced them to another line. Only a teenager, a child, he screamed silently, in unbelievable fear, fear so terrible he was unable to raise one finger to save them. The soldiers shot anyone who tried to stop them. It didn't matter if there were a thousand witnesses staring in terror, the Nazis did what they pleased. The large dogs they held on thick leashes were always watching.

I shuddered at the pictures in my brain. They were more violent than anything on T.V. or in the movies I was allowed to see. The scenes were more frightening because they were real.

"And do you know what they did with the ones who couldn't work?" Grandpa's hands gripped the armrests of Dad's favorite chair as if he wanted to tear them apart.

"Dad! Sam! Please?" Mom was trembling, begging him to stop.

"Papa," Dad said. "Please, not yet."

Didn't Grandpa hear them? I wanted to cover my ears, but had to know. Whatever it was they hid from me couldn't be as bad as all the horrors I imagined, all the nightmares. I was wrong.

Grandpa trembled, his voice cracking. "The ones who were too old, too sick, too young to work…they gassed them… hundreds at a time…gassed them all. It was worse than what they do to animals." He burst into tears. "I lost them all. Robert, my dear boychick, do you understand? I lost every one of them…all…gassed like animals."

Oh my God! It can't be true! They 'gassed' human beings? Hundreds at a time? Nobody could be this cowardly, killing hundreds and hundreds of unarmed people with poison gas. I knew it was going to be horrible, but this? I never imagined. How could I?

Mom was sitting bolt upright, her hands locked on mine. There were tears running down her face, so I knew it was true. As impossible as it sounded, it was true.

Dad placed his hands on top of ours. I saw tears in his eyes too.

Grandpa's eyes were fierce. "They told them they was going to take showers. Can you imagine? So they undressed. And yes, it looked like a shower room,

even with fake showerheads. All to fool them. And then they gassed them…
hundreds and thousands of men, women, children…babies…my family."

"It's impossible! I don't believe you! How could they get away with
something like this? Nobody could kill so many people without being caught!
It's a lie!" Mom and Dad kept me from jumping up off the couch, wrapping
their arms around me, hugging me. "Nobody could have been this brutal.
How can it be true? How did other countries let something like this happen?
America would have stopped it!" I was screaming. I couldn't imagine this
nightmarish scene. I cried, unable to stop, my face buried in between my
parents. Sixth graders don't cry. But I did. I did.

Mom said, "David, it is true. I wish to God it wasn't, but it really happened
that way." She sighed. "I'm so sorry."

It took a while before I could look up.

Grandpa gave me a sad smile. "You are growing up, David," he said softly.
"No more my sweet, Duvidel. So I will tell you." He swallowed hard. "It is all
true. It really happened so."

"People don't do such things," I said, wishing I'd never heard any of it.

"Now you know why we didn't want to tell you," Dad said. "The Nazis
found a way to kill millions of people while the world didn't know or turned
their back. It was like a killing machine that wouldn't stop."

"But there had to be bodies," I said, thinking how on television crime shows
there were always bodies and clues. The murderers always got caught.

Mom whispered to Grandpa, "No. Not yet."

"Mom, I have to know," I said. What could be worse than what I already
found out? "Please? I need the truth…even if I hate it."

Mom nodded. "Rob, you tell him."

Grandpa sniffled. "Yes. It is fine. You should tell him. I am tired to death."

Dad looked at me and said softly, almost so low I couldn't hear, "David,
there is no easy way to tell you this." He looked at Mom.

Mom didn't move.

Dad sighed. "You asked about the bodies. So, I have to tell you. Okay?"

I nodded.

Dad looked at Mom again and said, "The Germans built ovens…"

"What? What did you say?"

Dad looked at Mom again. "David, they burned the bodies to ash, so nobody would know… then they buried the ashes… so, nobody would find them."

Grandpa weeped. His hands shook as he covered his face. "What kind of people do such things? What kind of monsters?"

Tears again. I couldn't think of anything to say. No words came from my lips. I wanted to make Grandpa feel better.

My father said gently, "Chris, take David upstairs." He walked over to Grandpa and wrapped his arms around him, whispering something I couldn't hear.

Grandpa's body was shaking against Dad, and he kept repeating, "Why? Why? Why?"

I felt a lump in my throat. I didn't want to leave, but Mom wrapped her arms around me in a hug. "Let Grandpa be for a little while. He'll be fine." She led me to the staircase. "Are you okay?" She rubbed my hair. "I'm sorry you had to hear all this. I tried to keep it from you as long as I could. Now, do you understand why we didn't want to tell you? It was horrible. I don't know what else to say. I'm so sorry."

I looked into her sad eyes. Mom was different from me. She was blond and blue-eyed, a Christian married to a Jew. She said she loved Dad and me. "Is it true, Mom? Is that what happened? Is that what they mean when they say they were 'exterminated?'" I understood it at last. It was just like Jeff's father's job. Only he killed millions of bugs and rodents, not humans. Humans exterminating other humans… millions and millions. It was like a horror movie, but it happened. Hitler got the Germans to exterminate millions of "dirty Jews" and too many others who they wanted to get rid of. 'Human trash.'

"I'm sorry, David," Mom repeated. "I love you, David, bigger than the whole world. Would you like me to come upstairs with you?"

The truth was I wanted to stay with Grandpa, to make sure he wasn't going to have another heart attack. "Is Grandpa okay?"

Mom gave me a kiss on the cheek. "Yes. He is here, where he belongs."

In my room, after Mom left, I lay on my bed staring at the ceiling. The pictures in my brain of all those lost souls wouldn't let me sleep. Mom said it was all true. I still couldn't believe it. The numbers were incredible. What the Nazis did was a horror story.

I pulled out my social studies book and turned to the index. There was only one mention of the Holocaust, only a few pages about World War II, near the end of the book. I remembered what Mrs. Goldstein said, and wondered if we would get to it by the end of the year. I thought about the short, strange, entry about the Holocaust on the school's dedicated network. I couldn't understand how something that changed so many lives, something that was still hurting so many families even now, could wind up being compressed into one or two short paragraphs. It was as if the subject wasn't important. It was as if it never happened, or they wanted to make believe it never happened. I don't know. I was only eleven years old, and this was way too much mystery for someone so young to solve.

As I tried to get to sleep, I couldn't erase the picture of my Grandfather, a little older than me at the time, standing on a long line, exhausted, hungry, cold and afraid. Suddenly, his Mama, Papa, baby brothers and sisters, were torn away from him. Imagine the panic. Where are they? Where are they? You want to scream and cry. But always nearby, rifles ready, are the soldiers whose faces I saw as icy masks, twisted by hate and the sick joy of seeing others tortured and killed.

Mom was right. I had nightmares. But, at least, I finally knew the true story and would make sure it was not forgotten.

Once upon a time, there lived a large and happy family in Poland. It was a family that never hurt anyone, but nobody would ever find out how they died… nobody would ever see their pictures again…their faces. Grandpa was right. It was as if they never existed at all. The Nazis vowed to erase every trace of their lives, every record of their history, their existence. They almost succeeded by killing millions of innocent people. Thankfully, they failed. Grandpa was alive. And I was alive to tell the story they wanted buried with the ashes.

This family once lived in a building in a city in Poland. It was a small apartment house they worked hard to buy, and for which they felt great pride.

The Nazis stole even this, their precious home. Now it was being kept from the last survivor by the Polish government that took over once Germany was defeated. It was this building, our family home, for which my Grandfather had been fighting. And it was this house that I wanted him to have back. More than anything I ever wanted, before or since, I wanted my Grandfather, Samuel Abraham Jacobovitz, son of Rachel and Max Jacobovitz, to have the satisfaction of standing in his house, laughing at all those monsters who tried to destroy every memory of our family. This building I had never seen was the only thing left of our past. Nobody else should have it. Nobody.

The following morning, I was surprised to see Dad fully dressed, but he hadn't gone to his accounting office. I walked over to Mom. "Is Dad sick? Isn't he going to work?"

"No, sweetheart, not today," Mom replied, placing her arm around my shoulder.

I looked again.

Dad was sitting next to Grandpa who was speaking on the phone in Polish. For once Grandpa wasn't shouting. Dad was telling him in English what to say, and Grandpa was translating it into Polish.

Mom pointed.

I looked.

Grandpa's hand was resting on top of Dad's.

As I walked to the bus stop, I had a secret. Dad never loses an argument. Like Mom says, once he makes up his mind, nothing stops him. Seeing him with my stubborn old Grandpa, "the stubbornest old man ever," I knew the Polish government wouldn't know what hit them. It would be cool to go to Hawaii, but I couldn't wait to tell Mr. Hernandez, Principal Robinson, and Mrs. Goldstein, that in a few months, we would be going to see our home in Poland, and nobody would ever take it away from us again.

Well, that's what I thought.

CHAPTER 27

I t took many more months of hard work, but one day, when I got home from school, Grandpa was happier than I ever saw him. "Hoo, hoo, hoo! I have such news!"

Grandpa was dressed in a white button-down shirt and good pants. Most days when I got home I found him in his old blue robe and worn brown slippers, watching television. Sometimes he looked like a zombie. All he did was watch T.V., but not today. "I feel wonderful," he said, almost dancing out of Dad's favorite chair which was now definitely his. "Do you want to hear a secret, my wonderful, Duvidel?"

I had a lot of homework in sixth grade, but seeing Grandpa happy was more important than anything. "Sure. What's up, Grandpa?"

"It is done. It is finally done."

"What is?" I thought he was flipping out.

"It is ours again." Grandpa had tears in his eyes. "You don't understand? David, your brilliant Papa did it! Mama and Papa would be so proud of him." He pulled me into his arms, and for a few seconds, he felt strong again. I let him hug me for as long as he wanted, still not understanding what changed him so much, praying it would last.

Dad walked in. "What's up you two? Did someone have a great test score today? David? A+?"

"Are you sitting?" Grandpa asked Dad.

It didn't take a detective to see Dad was standing.

Dad looked alarmed. "Not another heart attack?" He looked at me. "Is your Grandfather okay?"

"No. No. I feel wonderful, my brilliant son." Grandpa laughed.

"Thank Goodness for that." Dad put down his briefcase. "Okay, so what's happening?" He winked at me. "I know you two. What have you got cooking? A surprise for your mother?"

"Are you ready?" Grandpa was like a little kid. He was so excited.

"Come on, Papa. What are you up to?" Dad looked at me.

I wasn't ratting. I still wasn't sure what was going on.

"Alright, here it is. This is yours. You deserve it." Grandpa handed a large brown envelope to Dad.

I saw Grandpa had torn it open.

Dad turned the envelope over. "You know I can't read Polish, Papa," Dad said, examining the return address.

"So I'll tell you, Boychick." It meant "little boy" and was a sign of affection. "I knew with your help we would do it. I knew! I knew!"

"What are you talking about?" Suddenly, Dad's face changed to a look of amazement. "You're kidding? We won? We really won after all these years?" He pulled the letter from the envelope even if he couldn't understand it. "Oh, Dad, really? I'm so happy for you. You wanted this so much. I thought it was impossible. I honestly thought it was a lost cause."

"I wanted this for our family." Grandpa wiped tears from his face. "And you did it. You did it."

"I thought it was crazy," Dad said, "I didn't believe it was possible, not after so many years." He stretched out his hand to shake Grandpa's hand.

"A handshake? Are you mashugah, my brilliant son?" Grandpa laughed and pulled Dad into his arms. "You make me so happy. You make all of our family proud."

Dad wiped tears from his face. "So the house is yours at last. I'm really happy for you, Papa. You never gave up. You deserve it." He gave his father a kiss on the cheek. "I can't believe the house is yours after more than sixty years. It's a miracle."

Grandpa released Dad from his hug. "It is God. I told you. Now, maybe you believe."

"Maybe you're right," Dad said, "I never thought this would happen."

And I never thought I'd hear my father admit that God may exist. I thought about that a lot lately. I also thought about learning more about being Jewish. Grandpa said that having even a tiny drop of Jewish blood in me meant to a Hitler that no matter how hard I try, I will always be branded as a Jew." People who no longer thought of themselves as Jewish were shocked when they were rounded up with other Jews. As Grandpa said, "They could scream bloody murder that they weren't Jewish, but the soldiers took them anyway. Imagine dying without your faith?"

After all the stories of what happened to my family just because they were Jewish, I was beginning to understand that to someone who hated Jews, I would always be a Jew. Even Mom, married to a Jew, sealed her fate under a monster like Hitler. It would be wrong not to learn more about the religion of my ancestors, even if I was only half Jewish.

Grandpa was dancing by his chair holding Dad's hands. "It is a miracle! There are details, but yes, my parents' home is ours at last. Thank you, my dear son. Thank you, God. Amen."

"What details?" Dad asked, still smiling, but no longer dancing. "What details, Papa?"

"Just some details," Grandpa said, dropping back into the chair. "This is natural after sixty years. You expect problems."

Dad's expression drooped. "Papa, what problems? Is there something wrong? What aren't you telling me?"

Grandpa looked guilty, just like I do when I try to hide something from Mom or Dad. "Why the worried face, boychick? It is nothing. Just a few things to work out."

"I know you, Papa. There is something you're not telling me."

Grandpa looked down at his slippers. "It is just that the building was taken over by the Polish government after the war. You know this."

"That shouldn't be a problem. The Polish Government gave it up. Right?"

"Yes. The Polish government is giving it back, now that our Polish lawyer has put in all the right papers, thanks to your smartness, which God gave to you."

"So, problem solved. Or isn't it?"

I thought Dad was too suspicious. Why did he have to question such a happy event? Grandpa finally had his building back. That was amazing.

"Papa, I want the truth right now," Dad said, staring down at Grandpa.

Grandpa sighed. "There are families living in our building."

"That's good," Dad replied. "The rent will come in handy. We'll pay back the lawyer and—"

"These families don't pay rent."

"What do you mean?"

"They don't pay rent." Grandpa shrugged his shoulders.

"They're living in the house for free?" Dad twisted the envelope, not a good sign.

"Yes."

"For how long?"

"Years. The lawyer says he tries to get them to pay, but they don't."

Dad fell into a seat on the couch. "You've got to be kidding. This is not a small detail, Papa."

Grandpa sighed again. "It gets worse."

"How can this get any worse?"

Grandpa gave me a look that said watch out for the explosion. "The lawyer says the Polish government transferred ownership to us five months ago."

"Five months? We owned this building five whole months and didn't know it?"

"Things take time in Poland, the lawyer explains. There is much red tape. Papers had to be filled out and mailed back and forth, and back and forth, and—"

Dad looked worried. "But this will be all straightened out soon?"

"The lawyer says yes, now that we turned off the electricity, hot water and heat."

That was all Dad had to hear. "WHAT?" The explosion could be heard around the world, even in Poland.

CHAPTER 28

And that is how when summer vacation came, two years after that first phone call, we ended up on a deserted, dusty, Polish street. A trio of grown men standing outside, arguing about a building that looks as if it is ready to be torn down. It belongs to us, 'lock, stock and cockroaches.' Oh, yes, and squatters, people who pay nothing to live here and won't leave.

The building looks haunted. I hope the ghosts are the spirits of Grandpa's family, not the evil spirits of their brutal murderers.

I stare at the building where I'll pick up the final pieces of my family's terrifying mystery. Dust makes the bricks of the apartment building, across the street, look gray. The bottom windows are covered by wood boards.

"Is this really it, Grandpa?" A detective, even a twelve-year old one, isn't supposed to be afraid, but I know this building's past. This is where my family was murdered.

"It does not look like much," Grandpa mutters in his thick Polish accent, not getting out of the car. There is a weary expression on his face as he studies the building he dragged us across the ocean to see. He pulls his ankle-length gray coat tighter around his frail body. The long airplane flight took a lot out of him, Dad said.

Mr. Moroski, the Polish lawyer, picked us up at the hotel and drove us here. He wears a black coat covering a black suit with faded white stripes. He also wears a maroon, narrow, neck tie, and brown laced shoes which need polishing. His slicked-back black hair and wire-thin moustache, make him look like a gangster from Grandpa's old movies. He bends to offer Grandpa a hand out of the car.

"I don't need your help." Grandpa grips the top of the car door and pulls himself up.

Moroski carries a badly scratched leather briefcase. It is large enough to hide a gun. "I called the police," he says in his broken English, glancing up the block. He looks like a nervous weasel.

I don't trust him. I don't trust anyone here. I know the truth.

"Why do we need police," Dad asks.

"The people here might do you harm," the lawyer replies.

Haven't they done enough to us, I think to myself, as I straighten my Yankee team cap.

"Sometimes I wish I did not start this," Grandpa grumbles, leaning on his cane.

"I warned you," Dad replies. "You wouldn't listen to me. You never do."

"I said, sometimes, but now I take it back. I am not sorry at all. Right is right!" Grandpa turns to talk to the lawyer in Polish.

"It looks haunted," I whisper to Dad. "I didn't expect it to look so bad." It really looks like a perfect hiding place for ghosts, an old rotten building, piles of garbage scattered in the alley, and graffiti on the walls. "What do you think that writing on the wall says?"

Dad shoots it a disgusted look. "Who cares? We own this dump, lock, stock and cockroaches."

"It wasn't like this when I was a boy," Grandpa says. "Mama and Papa was so proud of it."

Proud of this? I'd burn it to the ground if Grandpa didn't want it so bad. I zip up my blue jacket, feeling a chill, nothing to do with the weather.

Grandpa frowns. "Moroski says inside is even worse." He spits on the ground and hisses, "They're a bunch of thieves and murderers. I could kill them all."

Grandpa scares me when he talks like that. I don't like how angry his face gets. It's as if he's a different person. I'm afraid he'll have another heart attack.

The lawyer looks at his watch again. "We go in. I have other appointments. The police catch up…if they get here at all."

No police? We're going inside? Moroski said they might hurt us. All my instincts are screaming, this is a trap.

CHAPTER 29

We're across the street from the building that Grandpa fought to get returned to him for many years. I hate it. The lawyer wants to take us inside even though the police are nowhere in sight. This boarded-up apartment house on a deserted street is perfect for an ambush.

"David, this is not a good area." I think Dad reads my mind.

The buildings here look like they're falling apart, decay and garbage that you don't see in the better parts of the city near our hotel. The alley next to the building is over-grown with weeds. A wire fence fell down, so the trash in the empty lot next door, which looks as if one time it was hit by a bomb, over-flows onto our property. This whole place is a mess. I can't wait to get back to our hotel, and then, home.

The lawyer, Moroski, looks at his watch again, and says, "Sirs, I have no more time. I have other business. Please, let's go inside?"

Dad is snapping pictures of the front of the building. "Okay. David, you wait inside the car. You'll be safe there."

Grandpa shakes his head. "I want David should see our home—"

Dad turns to him. "We've come all the way to Poland for you, but I won't place my son in danger. You heard the lawyer. They might hurt us. Maybe later. After everything is settled." Dad shoots the lawyer an angry scowl. "How could you shut off their utilities? They're humans like us."

Are they human? I never could do what they did. No humans could have done that, only monsters.

"What, sir, are 'utilities?'" Moroski struggles with English.

116

"Heat, water and electricity," Dad replies angrily.

"Ah. Yes. These peoples pay no rent. For years they live here and pay not one dollar," Moroski replies. "Do you want to pay forever for them? Is this what you wish?" Do you want to pay forever?"

Dad grumbles, "No wonder they hate us. I'd hate us if I had no water, lights, and had to shiver in the cold because the lawyer for my new American landlords shut off everything."

Moroski shut off their heat, electricity and water? The squatters are stuck in the cold without heat, lights, and water? Good. Why should I care about them? Did they care about what they did to us?

"David, your Grandfather has gotten us into a terrible mess," Dad says, looking disgusted.

"So, this is my fault?" Grandpa's face shows he's about to erupt again.

"You wanted your revenge. Now look what you've done to us."

"I am only taking back what is ours," Grandpa rasps, his accent stronger because he's upset. "They stole everything from us. You will never understand! You don't care they murdered our whole family."

Moroski hisses, "Please. This is not right to say. They will hear."

I was shocked the first time Grandpa said 'murder,' but I've heard him say it so many times since this started, that I'm used to it. I didn't believe him at first. Now, every time I think of what happened to our family, I get so mad I want to kill everyone in this awful building...everyone in this country.

"It was them and the Germans," Grandpa shouts, glaring at Dad. His eyes are so full of anger that it looks as if Grandpa hates Dad too.

Dad frowns. "It wasn't these people, Papa. It was a long time ago. It's in the past."

"Not for me," Grandpa slams back. "And it should not be for you! Not for David neither."

"I don't want to argue again with you here. I still can't believe that lawyer shut off their heat, power and water? How can he let children freeze? Papa, he works for you. Please tell Mr. Moroski to restore everything now? Papa, you tell him, or I will."

"No you won't," Grandpa says, grabbing my father's arm.

"Grandpa, be careful!" I'm afraid he'll have another heart attack. He promised the doctor he would stay calm or Dad would never have let him take this trip. As if he could stop him. They're both stubborn mules.

Dad pulls easily away from Grandpa's fingers and rushes toward the lawyer who is barking into a phone. "Mr. Moroski, I need to talk to you."

I hope Moroski is calling the police.

"Robert, wait!" Grandpa hurries to catch Dad, swinging his cane ahead of each step.

"What do you want? I've had enough of this." Dad looks ready to tangle with that lawyer and the whole Polish army.

Grandpa holds up a shaky hand. He's wheezing. "Robert. Listen. It wasn't Moroski. It was me. I told him to do it."

Dad freezes in his tracks. "You? You told him?" Dad stares at Grandpa like he doesn't know him. "How could you do that? All this time, I thought it was the lawyer. It was you?"

I was shocked. I thought it was the lawyer too. Hey, Grandpa was pretty smart to cut off their heat, water and lights until they either pay or got out. These are the people who stole our house in the first place. They helped the Germans destroy my family. And now, they don't pay rent?

Grandpa's breathing hard. "They was paying no rent and…they won't leave. We can't pay for them forever—"

"So, you shut off everything?" Dad looks as if he's having the heart attack this time.

"It's our home! They have no right—"

Dad hisses so Moroski can't hear. "Are you insane? What were you thinking? Just look how they live here. This is a slum! Nobody should live like this! And you turn off everything? I don't believe it. I just don't believe you could do something like this."

"They force me. They don't understand anything else." Grandpa's face is twisted with anger.

I'm afraid he's having another attack.

"Papa, they are people," Dad says in a pleading voice. "People! How could you do this? What is wrong with you?"

118

Grandpa's face is ugly, his eyes narrow, his voice raspy. "I hate them. They destroyed my whole family and left us nothing. Why should we care about them? They cared nothing for us. I spit on them all."

I don't like the way Grandpa sounds and looks when he's angry like this, but I think he's right. These Polish monsters hurt us so much that we have the right to get even. He is entitled to his revenge. We all are. But I'm terrified Grandpa's going to have another attack. "Dad," I risk being yelled at for butting-in, "Please stop? Look at Grandpa's face."

Dad glances at me and then turns back to Grandpa. "Papa, please listen to me? These poor people here didn't do it. They weren't even born then. The ones who did these horrible things are dead, or dying. It's over. Papa, it's over."

"It will never be over. I will never forget. God forbid. Never!"

"Papa, I'll never forget either. Nobody should forget. But you survived Auschwitz, where there was no heat, no hope, no compassion. How can you, a survivor of all that horror, do this to others?"

Grandpa explodes, waving his cane in the air. "You dare throw Auschwitz at me?"

How can Dad compare what the Germans did in Auschwitz, a death camp, to what Grandpa is doing to get these people to either pay rent or get out of our house? It is our house and the lawyer says the law is on our side.

Moroski stops talking on his phone, staring at Grandpa and Dad arguing in the street.

I wish they'd stop. It's horrible. I hate these Polish people for what my Grandfather looks like, rage twisting his face into an ugly mask, eyes smoldering and lips trembling. One of his hands is wrapped tightly around the cane, which is still in the air, shaking in fury. "You can't understand! You wasn't there! You didn't see your parents and eight brothers and sisters murdered. You didn't see your poor mother starving and coughing with the icy cold, and sickness, which took her from me. My Esther. These monsters let this happen. They told the Germans where we was hiding. They wanted everything from us."

Dad lowers his voice. "Some Polish did inform the Nazis and were

119

rewarded with our property, but others fought against the Germans—"

"They raised not one finger to stop it. Nobody stopped it. They are all guilty. Their children and grandchildren, all guilty. All." Grandpa slams the rubber tip of the cane on the ground and storms across the road, toward the three concrete steps that lead to the graffiti-scarred front of the apartment house. "I will deal with these vermin myself. I don't need you for this," he growls and disappears into the dark doorway.

Dad looks as if he doesn't know what to do. "I can't believe your Grandfather could do this. All this time I thought it was the lawyer who got us in this mess." He lets out a curse. "That old fool will get himself killed if they find out. Stay inside the car! You'll be safer out here! I won't be long."

"Dad, I don't want to wait here. I want to go home." I don't even want to be a detective anymore.

"Please, David? Wait in the car. I have no idea what it's like inside. I'll talk some sense into your crazy Grandfather or let these people do what they want with him." He runs toward the building.

Moroski shouts some curse in Polish, and runs after him, holding his briefcase against his chest.

I hope there's a gun in there. Just in case. But then Moroski might turn it on us. He's one of them.

All three are gone, sucked up in that awful building, a building crawling with inhuman monsters. Will they really hurt us? Do they hate us that much?

I know Grandpa hates them. He can hardly speak when he says they murdered his whole family. Now that I've solved the whole terrifying mystery, I want them to suffer too…just like they made my family suffer…my Grandpa and Nana.

I'm afraid to follow into the building, and Dad ordered me to stay inside the car. Anything can happen out here. I pull the rear passenger door handle. It doesn't open. I try the other doors. "Oh, my God! They're all locked! Moroski locked me out of his car!"

CHAPTER 30

I run around and try all the car doors again. "Locked! Great!" Moroski's car is sitting here like a big black fortress and I'm locked out! Did he think I was going to steal it? He probably thinks all Americans are criminals if he watches our old shows, now on their T.V.s. It was funny seeing American cops and crooks talking in a foreign language. Their mouths moving don't match the words.

This street would be a great place to film a gangster movie. I can imagine the trash-strewn lot next to our building as the scene of a bloody gunfight. Moroski, with his greasy-looking hair, black moustache, and that horrible black striped suit, is perfect for the gang chief. I see him holding a machine gun and, "rat-a-tat-tat! Drop dead, you dirty Jew!"

Moroski. I don't like that lawyer guy. First, he's Polish, and from everything Grandpa told me about them; they can't be trusted. Second, I don't like the way he looks, with his long black coat, and always carrying that black leather briefcase. And now, to top it all off, he locked me out of his car, so I'm stuck on this creepy street waiting for Dad and Grandpa to come out of that even creepier building. Why did we have to come here in the first place?

This darn building. It's why I'm here and not in Hawaii. This stupid, broken-down, building, with its boarded-up windows, that Grandpa has been fighting to get back, is why I was left out here in the street. Anything can happen. Mom would yell 'bloody murder' at Dad for leaving me alone like this. I guess he didn't know that 'Moron-ski,' (Moroski-moronski? That's funny.) locked up his precious car. I'll bet that lawyer did it on purpose.

When Grandpa first explained why he wanted to come here, I didn't understand. Even now, looking at this place, with its unfriendly squatters wrecking it, I don't want this dump, and neither does Dad. Weeks after Dad gave in and said we would go with Grandpa to Poland, they got into one of their 'fights.' Mom was in the kitchen and Grandpa was sitting in Dad's favorite chair. Dad was sitting on the couch staring at Grandpa.

I thought maybe Dad wanted his old chair back.

Dad picked up the remote. Without warning, he muted the television. "Papa, I need to talk to you."

"Now? In the middle of my show? Why do you always interrupt at the best part?"

"Papa, please?"

"Okay, so what is it so important you need to interrupt my only pleasure in life?"

"Papa, I know you've been trying to get back this building forever, but honestly, is it worth it? You're making yourself sick again. What are you going to do with an apartment house in Poland?" He lowered his voice. "You know they killed some Jews who went there to take back their property. Do we really need to do this?"

Grandpa's face got dark as it always did when they discussed Poland. "You know it is not the building. It is the principle."

"Not that again." Dad looked at me. "David, do you know what 'principle' means?"

"He's Mr. Robinson, the head of my school," I replied.

Grandpa laughed. "No, Duvidel. That is a different principle. This 'principle' is something I am fighting for." He looked at Dad. "That is the trouble with English. One word has too many meanings. I'm here almost sixty years and I still don't understand your crazy language."

"Papa, they are spelled differently. David, the 'principal' you are thinking of, ends with p-a-l. The 'principle' Grandpa is referring to, ends with p-l-e."

"What does it matter," Grandpa barked. "It just makes it difficult. It's a crazy language with three different ways to spell one word: 'two,' 'to,' and 'too.' Mashugah."

"And don't forget 'tu-tu,'" I added, trying to defuse this discussion before it exploded into another argument.

"What is this 'tu-tu?'" Grandpa looked confused.

"Never mind. It isn't important." Dad gave me an annoyed look. "I guess the best way to explain what Grandpa's 'principle' means is that it is an idea you believe in very strongly."

"Yes," Grandpa interrupted. "Like I said, something you would fight for, something what is the most important to you."

Dad sat down on the couch again. "In this case, it isn't how much the building is worth in money, but what it means to your Grandfather—"

Grandpa cut in, "Not to me only! It should mean the same to you."

Oh, oh! We were sitting on dynamite again. Grandpa was lighting the fuse.

Dad quickly said, "Papa. it does mean the same to me. I just don't want you to get sick again from it. No principle is worth that."

Grandpa straightened up. "This one is. Even if I have to die for it, I will not stop fighting until I take back what the 'rats' took from us like we did not exist." He turned to me. "David, I have waited all my life to stand again in my parents' house, and say it is ours again. Do you understand?"

I nodded.

Grandpa glared at Dad. "Nobody will take that away from me again. Nobody."

"He's as stubborn as these car door locks," I grumble, still not believing I'm stuck out here, in this slum, where any slimy 'rat' can attack. So much for principles. I just want to go home.

Why don't they come out already? It seems like they've been in there for hours. I wish the police would come. I miss Mom.

Dad says I should give these Polish people a chance. "People are people," he says, but Grandpa hates them so much. Even the lawyer, and he's one of them, is afraid they might hurt us. The few Polish people I've met in the hotel look at you funny when they realize you're not Polish. Maybe they suspect we're Jews. Mom said a lot of people, even today, don't like Jews. We're even. I don't like the Polish either. When I look at them, all I can think about is that their parents, or grandparents, were here when all the bad things happened. Were they part of it? Grandpa blames them all. He says those who did nothing are just as bad as those who did the killing and stealing. Am I as guilty as Tony because I didn't try and stop him from bullying Joseph that day?

"Darn Poland!" *Our summer vacation money had to go for this trip, and I'm alone here, waiting by a locked car, instead of on a beach in Hawaii.* "That's it! I'm going in. It's gotta be better than waiting out here."

There are five pigeons on the roof of the building. They look like black vultures, big and ugly. "I guess we own them too, "lock, stock, cockroaches," and now 'vultures?'"

I'm about to cross the street when something catches my eye. A door in the side of the building is opening. Someone is walking out.

Why is he so walking so close to the wall? Is he looking around? Maybe he won't see me. Wait! He's coming this way! I try the driver door again. Damn that Moroski.

The stranger is dressed in a dark jacket and cap. He's carrying something. It's a long stick.

CHAPTER 31

Dad wanted me to sit in Moroski's big black car, but the lawyer locked it. Now some guy in dark clothing and carrying a stick, is walking toward me. Normally, I wouldn't be afraid, but this is Poland, and Grandpa's history scared me about the people that live here. Now, I'm afraid of them.

I'd run to the building into which Grandpa and Dad have disappeared, but this guy can easily cut me off. One shot of that stick...

Moroski, said he called the police. Did he lie about that? Is he in on this? Is it all a big trap? Are Dad and Grandpa tied up somewhere in this darn building that lured us here like stupid fish to a hook?

Okay, I'm being dramatic, but I am locked out of Moroski's car, facing some character in dark clothes, carrying a huge stick. And, I've nowhere to run.

I look at the front door of Grandpa's building across the street, praying I'll see Dad rushing out. I'm too far away to yell for help and my phone is dead here. I'm really stuck. I swing my eyes to the other corner of the building. Is someone going to jump me from that side too?

I remember Grandpa saying he wasn't a hero. Mom, who never acted like she liked him, told me he was very brave. He risked his life to carry messages and food through the sewers. For a second, I think of ducking under a manhole cover into a sewer, but no way can I lift it. And, I hate rats.

The figure across the street looks like a killer in my horror movies, dressed all in black, a dark cap hiding his hair and eyes. He's carrying that stick in his right hand. I should be relieved he isn't some big tough guy with a

125

machinegun, but I'm not. Moroski warned us, "The people here might do you harm." I wish I was brave like Grandpa.

"I'm no hero," Grandpa said that morning in the kitchen. "I was always afraid. The nightmares still make me afraid."

The nightmares just from his story were enough to frighten me. Who wouldn't be afraid after hearing what happened to the Jews who lived here… to my family, the family I never knew because they were all murdered.

"How did you get over being afraid?" I asked. I felt like a coward. I didn't want to tell anyone, not him, not Dad, and especially not Mom, that I was having nightmares about the Nazi soldiers smashing down doors. They would never let me hear the rest of the story. I had to hear it even if I was scared.

Grandpa smiled sadly. "Duvidel, I did not get over it. I am still afraid."

"You don't show it."

"I work hard to not to show I am afraid." He looked at me before he spoke again. "You know, David, you can learn much from books. A smart man, smarter than me even." He laughed. "Anyway, this very smart man, William Shakespeare, once said something like, "The coward dies a thousand times, but the brave die once." Do you understand what this means?"

"No idea." I heard from some older kids that Shakespeare was boring. It shows you shouldn't listen to what other kids say.

Grandpa smiled. "I did not know what this means at first either. I think it means when a man is afraid of death, it is like dying many times. My English is not so good. I hope I explain this right to you."

I never thought about death much before this whole thing started. Who does when you're a kid? "I think I understand. You imagine what dying is like, and that is like feeling it for real. Is that it?"

"Yes. That is it, my brilliant grandson. You imagine how it will hurt, and, so, it is like feeling that pain over and over."

"That's awful."

Grandpa nodded. "Yes. So, the trick is, you make yourself not afraid. This is very hard to do. But if you can, you will feel the pain only once." He smiled and repeated, "A coward dies a thousand deaths."

"I think I get it. That Shakespeare was pretty smart. Like before I go to the dentist, I'm so afraid that I imagine the pain over and over. The real pain is never as bad…usually. I get it." I looked at Grandpa. "Is that what you did when you were afraid?"

"I wasn't smart enough in those days to think of this idea myself. I didn't read Shakespeare until I live in Florida. I wish I knew this then. I always try to remember now. I try not to be afraid."

"I try too, but it doesn't always work."

"Not for me neither. In those terrible days, nothing could make me not afraid, but I had to do what I could to survive. That is what we must always do. We must survive."

"I would have been terrified," I said, wondering if he told me that Shakespeare thing because he knew I was a coward.

"I was terrified too. Sometimes, when you are facing danger you must simply face it right back. There is no running away. So, you must pretend to be brave. Like an actor in movies. It is your only hope. That and prayer. Prayer works too…even if your father doesn't believe so."

Before this trip to Poland, I was afraid. After Grandpa told me what these people did to my family, I worried they would try to hurt us too. I didn't want to show my fear because Grandpa wanted me to come with him so badly. I remember him sitting at the kitchen table, saying, "Duvidel, I want you to see my parents' home. I want you with me when it is ours again forever."

Dad had already told Mom he was going because he couldn't let Grandpa do this on his own, not after a heart attack. Mom said she would have gone too if Grandpa Jack wasn't becoming so forgetful. She had to go to Boston to help them move him into an assisted living, where she says he'll get the help he needs. I wish she was here with me. I wish I was there with her. Dad gave me a choice, but I wanted to be with my Grandpa when he finally won against the Polish who stole our house. So that's how I got here.

The stranger is across the street.

If I stay hidden behind Moroski's car and he spots me, he'll know I'm afraid. He looks taller than me. That stick looks like it can do damage. "Sometimes there is no running away." I hear Grandpa's voice in my brain.

I wish I could see the stranger's face, but the cap is covering it. Does he know I'm here? Has he come for me?

"The coward dies a thousand times." I want to believe what Grandpa said. Even though I'm terrified, I force myself to stand tall. *I'm not afraid. I'm not afraid.*

Suddenly, I am hit with a flashback of a large boy beating up someone. The victim tries to defend himself as a crowd of kids, all shadows, do nothing to help him. He is punched hard in the stomach and falls to the ground. The crowd, now all with my face, stands by as the older boy, eyes filled with hate, Hitler's blazing eyes, screams, "Drop dead, you dirty Jew!"

I hear the others join in the chant. "Drop dead, you dirty Jew! Drop dead, you dirty Jew!"

"Run away. Be safe," a voice inside my head screams. "Run. Run away!"

The boy on the ground lifts his face. Even through the blood I see... my eyes staring up at me as if asking, "Why did you not do anything?" I reply, "I did. But Jeff was there, and so were my other friends to back me up. Who is here to help me? This time, I'm alone."

CHAPTER 32

The stranger is still on his side of the street. What is he waiting for? Why doesn't he come for me?

I made up my mind to be brave, like Grandpa. It is easier to 'decide' to be brave than to actually do it. Do I have a choice? If I stay here and he sees me hiding he'll know I'm petrified of him. That's a sure invitation to a beating.

He still isn't moving.

Enough! Pretending I'm not afraid of him, I walk to the front of the long black hood of Moroski's car. I'd try a run to the building, but I can't make it before he whacks me with that stick.

Oh God! He sees me! He's looking around, probably checking if anyone's watching. *He's crossing over! He's coming this way!*

My hands are now fists. My eyes focus on the stick. It looks like a sawed-off broom handle, black tape wrapped around one end. The tape makes it easier to grip, easier to swing.

His lips form into a smile.

I think he looks like one of those killers in gangster movies Grandpa likes, smiling just before he shoots everyone dead. He has cold-looking blue eyes… not like Mom's, but killer cold.

"What do you want?" I hope my voice didn't crack. I try to keep my face hard and to look as tall as I can. I wish I was in a black jacket, anything to look tougher. Don't look like you're afraid, I tell myself.

He stops walking, staring at me, sizing me up.

What am I a creature from space or something?

"Rosumye Propolski?"

I don't like the sound of Polish even when Grandpa speaks it. I don't understand any of it, and don't want to. "I don't speak Polish," I say, wishing he would leave me alone.

He looks puzzled and says something else I don't understand.

"I told you I don't speak Polish." I want to say, "I don't speak to no rotten Poles," but I don't want to provoke him. He looks like he can take me with one hand tied behind his back, especially with that stick. I'm in a lot of trouble here. Where's Dad when I need him?

"Americanski?"

I nod. Does he hate Americans too?

"I no speak Englisher good," he says with a worse accent than Grandpa. "German? Sprecken zie Deutch?"

I shrug my shoulders. "No German." *Definitely not German.*

I jump backwards when he swings the stick in the air. *What the hell is he doing?* I hear the swoosh of the stick and feel the air rushing toward me. I must look frightened because he stops swinging the stick and says, "Vilst speil mit mir?"

I have no idea what language he is talking, or what he is saying, and I don't want to know. I just want Dad and the U.S. Army to save me from this stupid Pole and his stick. I want to go home.

The stranger takes off his cap. He has thick blond hair. He shakes his head and says something else I don't understand. He digs into his jacket pocket.

Is he going for a knife? A gun? This is crazy! What am I doing out here with someone who might pull a gun on me? The heck with it! I'm going to make a run for the building.

He drops something from his hand and I automatically catch it.

It is a rubber ball. This jerk wants me to play ball with him? Do I want to play with him? He's a Pole. He's one of the people who did horrible things to my family. Okay, he didn't, but his parents or grandparents did. I shake my head and drop the ball into his hand. How can I play with someone whose parents or grandparents could have been murderers? Just living in Grandpa's building for so many years, not paying rent, makes them all crooks, and for all I know, Jew-haters. He could be like his parents and grandparents who beat up Jews and forced them out of their homes. "No," I say, afraid of him. "I don't want to play with you. No!"

The boy looks disappointed for a minute, but then waves his hand for me to follow him.

I shake my head.

He replaces the hat on his head. His hand reaches toward me.

"Get away from me! I don't want to play with you. Leave me alone, you dirty Pole!" I hear someone shouting, "Dirty Jew!" Did I say that? Did I calll him that?

The boy looks confused.

I don't care. I don't care anything about him or anyone else in this horrible building. Did they care about us? Please, just get away from me?

Why doesn't he leave? Why is he still here, staring at me with hurt eyes? He must know I don't want to talk to him. What is he thinking about? What is he going to do to me? Did he understand what I called him? I'm not sorry. I'm scared. Did I get him angry enough to hurt me? I wish I had a weapon… a gun.

CHAPTER 33

I hate everything about this place that had an Auschwitz, and a ghetto with dead-looking buildings, and heartless people. People? I thought of them as little more than cold-blooded thieves and murderers.

I didn't want to see the apartment house that was once our family's home. Grandpa said I would regret not taking this once-in-a-lifetime chance, so I came with him in Moroski's car, away from the safety of our hotel. He drove us in his fancy automobile to this 'bad' part of the city that had been a corral for hundreds of thousands of Jewish families. No Jews live here now. Auschwitz, and the other death camps, 'systematically exterminated' Jews from almost every country in Europe. Those that survived were scattered all over the planet, most staying far away from their former homes, the terrible memories that haunt every brick, every broken window.

When Grandpa stormed into our apartment house, after the argument with Dad, I was afraid of what the squatters might do to him. Would they welcome their new Jewish landlord with great big smiles? He took back the building the Nazis stole from our family sixty years ago and wanted them to pay rent. I was glad this would be the first and last time I'd ever see this country that was the site of our family's ashes and broken dreams.

I was shocked Moroski locked his car, trapping me in the street. I was frightened when a tall stranger began walking toward me carrying a long, black, stick. I was afraid of fighting him, just as was afraid of that bully beating up Joey and shouting, "Drop dead, you dirty Jew!" I did nothing to stop him. Now, I had no choice. I'm afraid, but this time I will not show my fear, not to one of these monsters.

The boy is looking at me, as if trying to figure out what kind of 'creature' I am before he makes a move. That makes us even. I have been trying to figure out what these people were who could do such terrible things to other human beings.

As he and I are sizing each other up, I realize I'm hurting someone too. He hasn't made a move against me. I'm the one filled with hate. All this boy wants to do is play ball with me, and I shouted at him...and we turned off their heat, water and electricity. I was happy about their misery. I wanted these people to suffer as my family suffered. I was thrilled Grandpa was getting his revenge at last. What happened to me? How can I be happy about hurting others?

"I can't believe that lawyer shut off their heat," my father had shouted as we faced the three story brick building. "How can he let children stay in a slum like this and freeze? Papa, tell Mr. Moroski to restore their electric, heat and water. Papa, you tell him or I will." He marched toward the lawyer who was barking into a phone in Polish.

"Wait, Robert," Grandpa shouted, rushing after him. "It wasn't Moroski. It was me. I told him to do it."

Dad turned to Grandpa. "You told him? You did this?"

I stared at Grandpa. It wasn't the Polish lawyer. It was him?

Dad's voice was a furious hiss. "How could you do that? All this time I thought it was the lawyer. But you? You could do something like this?"

"They was paying no rent and they won't leave. It's our home! They stole it from us! They have no right—"

"Are you insane? What were you thinking? Just look at how they live here. This is a slum. Nobody should live like this! And you turn off the heat, water, and electricity?"

"They force me to do it! They don't understand anything else these Polish rats."

"Papa, they're people," Dad said in a pleading voice. "People. How could you do this?"

Grandpa's face grew ugly, his eyes angry slits. "They're monsters. I hate them. I hate them for what they did to us. They destroyed my family and left us nothing. Why should we care about them? They cared nothing for us! I spit on them all!"

At the time, I thought Grandpa was right. They hurt us, so we had every right to get even. Sixty years is a long time to wait for revenge.

"Papa, these people didn't do it. It was Hitler and the Nazis. It was sixty years ago. It's over. Thank God, it is over."

"It will never be over. I will never forget. God forbid. Never. Never." Grandpa's face was twisted in anger.

Dad gazed into Grandpa's eyes. His voice was softer. "I will never forget either, Papa. But you were in Auschwitz, where there was no heat, no hope, no compassion. How can you, an Auschwitz survivor, do this to others?"

Grandpa screamed, "You dare throw Auschwitz at me?"

Moroski stopped talking on the phone, staring at Grandpa and Dad arguing in the street.

I wished they'd stop. I never saw Grandpa get so angry. I blamed the Nazis and the Poles for what he looked like, rage twisting the face I loved into an ugly mask. I was afraid of his eyes. They were smoldering. His hands were trembling fists. "You can't understand. You wasn't there. You didn't see your parents and eight brothers and sisters murdered! The Poles let this happen! They wanted everything from us! Nobody stopped it! They are all guilty!" Grandpa stormed toward the building holding his cane like a club.

Dad ran after him, afraid of what Grandpa might do and how the Poles in the building might react to their new Jewish landlord who cut off their services.

Moroski, the Polish lawyer, ran in after them, leaving me locked out of his car and facing this kid and this evil-looking, long, black, stick.

"I don't want to play with you," I had shouted, deliberately, wanting to hurt him. I applauded Grandpa depriving the Poles of heat, water and light. I never could have done that before. Can I really do this now? I felt sick at what I did, what I felt. The boy didn't understand what I yelled at him. Why I yelled at him.

The boy is still near, too near, looking confused.

I hurt him and I don't care. He is just a Pole, just a dirty Pole! Did I really say that? I sound like that bully, Tony. Am I that full of hate? I'm glad I can't see my face. Do I look like Grandpa, so full of hate?

The boy looks down the road and then back at me. "You Papa—he tell me— go see you. See you no be ...I not know how to say?" He shrugs, obviously struggling with English, unable to finish the sentence.

"My Papa sent you to see me?" I ask.

He smiles. "Yes, papa...you papa. He send me to you."

I realize he is trying hard to express himself in English, which is difficult for him. He is just a kid, taller and older than me, but still a kid. And he's trying hard to talk to me and I'm not helping. "My papa sent you?" I ask, a lot slower this time, as if he is deaf and I am helping him read my lips. I point to my chest. "My papa sent you?"

"Yes. You papa. He ask me... see you...safe. Yes?"

Dad sent him? Dad doesn't hate anyone, not even these Polish people. Mom gets mad sometimes because he's always so calm...well, most of the time, except for when he argues with Grandpa. I used to think it was because Dad didn't care about being Jewish and what happened to our family, but I know that isn't true. Dad is one of the most caring people ever. So how does he do it? How can he not hate these people? Why does he want Grandpa to stop hurting them, stop getting his revenge?

The boy startles me when he shouts, "Afraid." He gives me a big smile again. "You Papa want you not be 'afraid.' I say right? Yes? You no...afraid?"

I realize why this boy is here. I wish I could be more like Dad, especially after seeing how all this changed my Grandpa into someone I hardly recognize. I'm afraid of his face when he's angry. It reminds me of the cruel faces of the German soldiers in my nightmares. I don't like seeing him like that. I don't want to look like that. I don't want to feel like this anymore, so angry, so full of hate. All this fury bubbling inside me really is painful. I can't smile at this kid, but maybe I can be a little nicer. Can I? After all I've learned, I don't even know if I can stand being near them.

Is this what hate does to a person? How could the Nazis not feel anything doing such horrible things? As I stand on that Polish street, I realize what I need to do. I know what Mr. Hernandez would tell me to do. Can I?

CHAPTER 34

I'm still afraid of this boy because he's a Pole, but I'm more afraid of the way I've changed in the last few months. All he seems to want is for me to be friendly and I can't do it. Why not? It hurts being bottled-up with anger like this, so I have to try. "Yes," I say, "You said it right. 'a-fraid.'"

The boy moves his hand toward me very slowly, as if he is afraid of 'spooking' me again.

This time I don't back away, but look at the object in his hand. It is a rubber ball. "He only wants to play ball," I whisper to whichever of my family's ghosts are protecting me.

The boy bounces the ball in his palm.

What if it is a trick? These Poles are capable of anything. That's Grandpa talking. Is it me too?

The kid lifts the brim of his cap and smiles. "Base-ball," he says clumsily.

I understand him. I'm just not sure I want to have anything to do with him.

"Base-ball," he repeats, and drops the ball into my hand.

There is nobody else near. The ball in my hand is tempting. I am so bored standing around and waiting forever out here. What harm will it do? I don't have to like him to have a catch with him. He doesn't look like he wants to hurt me. I stood up to Tony and survived.

"Base-ball," he repeats.

Oh, why not? "I'm David." I point to myself. "Da-vid."

The boy looks puzzled for a second, then points to himself, and says, "Yanek. Ya-nek."

"Yankee?" I ask.

"Yankee?" The boy laughs and points at his black baseball cap. "Yes. I Yankee." He says it slowly, like the monster in that old Frankenstein movie. "Yon-kee. I like."

Yankee walks across the street, turns and waves for me to go with him.

I follow cautiously, a short distance behind. A good detective, I keep my eyes peeled on anywhere a bad guy might lurk in ambush.

In the alley between our building and the vacant lot, Yankee stops. He signals me to toss the ball. I do, and he tosses it back to me. After a few dozen throws, he moves farther back in the alley, but I stay near the front. I still won't take any chances. I want to be visible, just in case.

We play catch like that for a few minutes, by the building which was once Grandpa's home. It is now a slum in which Yankee lives without heat, water or electricity. Does he know it is my Grandfather who is responsible for their misery? Would he still want to play with me if he knew I was half Jewish?

After a while Yankee picks up the broom stick. He signals me to pitch to him.

I pitch underhand and he hits it. He hits them all. He is a much better hitter than me, but I'm only twelve, and he is at least fourteen or fifteen. Either that, or tall for his age.

Suddenly, Yankee misses the ball. He doesn't go after it. He is staring at the boarded-up window nearby, an alarmed look on his face.

Curious, I walk over and hear shouting inside. I try to understand what they are saying, but the shouting sounds inhuman, like a lot of loud squawking.

"Papa, stop this now!" I recognize Dad's voice breaking through the commotion. "These people are suffering because of us. It isn't right! How can we do this?"

The lawyer's broken English comes next. "I understand what you are feeling, sir, but you can't give in. They will never leave. You will pay for them forever. So will your children and grandchildren. Show you are strong. Do not surrender or you will never be rid of them."

Dad shouts back. "They're human beings for God's sake! We can't do to them what was done to us. Please Papa? For our family's sake, please end this? There has to be another way."

Several men are shouting in Polish again. They sound angry. And then I recognize Grandpa speaking loudly in English. "The lawyer is right, Robert. If I give in, these free-loaders will never leave. They force me to do this! It is their fault, not mine!"

"You're a stubborn mule," my father shouts.

The lawyer says something in Polish and there is more shouting.

That's all these Poles do, I think, bored with the whole business. I am about to turn away when I hear a loud bang. "Oh my God! A gunshot!"

CHAPTER 35

"Did you hear that? It sounded like a gun!" I shout to Yankee. Of course, he can't understand me, so he has a dumb look on his face. He holds his hand up and makes it look like his fingers are talking 'rapid fire.' He shakes his head and laughs. He's making fun of the adults arguing.

I make my hand into a gun and pull the trigger. "Bang! Bang! Don't you understand," I shout and run toward the building. "They shot someone," I call back at him.

"Bang? Bang?" Yankee repeats and follows me.

Forgetting about my safety I run up the front steps and pull open the door.

In the hallway, I stare in shock. The place is falling apart. Peeling paint, walls scarred by thick black smears, like Mom's eye make-up streaking down her face when she cries. The smells make me sick to my stomach. "This is disgusting! Do we really own this?" "Lock, stock and cockroaches." Dad's words echo in my brain. Why would anyone fight for a mess like this? It smells like dirty diapers. "Where are they?" I ask Yankee. "Where is my family?"

Yankee may understand. He signals me to follow him.

What choice do I have?

Yankee leads me to a dark stairway, the unpainted metal door corroding. It looks like someone pounded it with hammers. Why isn't the overhead light on? Grandfather! He cut off the electricity.

Yankee holds the door open.

No detective with common sense, would go down these dark stairs. "Can

I trust Yankee?" I hesitate. *Blond hair, blue eyes...he looks okay.* I know I am judging a book by its cover again...but he likes baseball. That should count for something. But trust a Pole? Can I do that? Both hands form into tight fists. I head down the stairwell. My heart is pounding. Any step may be a trap. It is dark. I can't see.

I am relieved when Yankee opens a metal door at the bottom of the stairs. I see light again, even if it is only the dim daylight filtering through the boarded windows from a room, door leaning uselessly against the wall. This place is a shambles. *How can people live like this? Why don't they just leave?* "Get out! Get out!" I hear the Nazi soldiers ordering everyone into the street. Why doesn't my Grandpa just throw them all out? I don't care about these people. I don't care if they are too poor to live anywhere else. I know nothing about them except they are the descendants of those that hurt my family. They are now living in our house, destroying our house, like rats. They're all rats.

The walls down here are like the rough concrete walls of our basement at home, or the rough surface of tombstones. That is not a pleasant thought in this place. *Yankee is gone. Where is he?*

I hear shouting. I must be close.

"I hope there aren't any real rats," I tell myself. The truth is I am more worried about 'human vermin,' the Polish species. I am sure they would shoot an old Grandfather and burn his body to ashes as the Germans did to millions of innocent people during the "systematic extermination" of the Holocaust. No wonder I am terrified. I hear Grandpa warning, "It can happen again."

Yankee is at the end of the hallway. He pushes open a steel door. He wants me to go in first. *Is he smiling? Is this a trap?*

I peer inside, always on guard.

At the far end of the room, lit only by the few rays of sun that penetrate the planked window, I see Grandpa, Dad, and the lawyer. They are surrounded by Poles. There are at least a dozen males and several women, a few holding small children by the hand. One woman has a baby pressed against her shoulder. Everyone looks angry, scowls on their faces. A few men are shouting at the same time. There are fists raised.

My grandfather has his stubborn face on. "Like a wall," Mom says when he gets like that. But at least he looks unhurt. Thank God.

But what about the gunshot? I look around. No gun. At least I don't see any.

Dad is glaring at the boiler. There aren't any flames or sounds coming from it. Grandpa cut off the fuel.

"Dad, are you okay?" I'm still at the door, afraid to enter.

Dad rushes over. "What are you doing down here? You were supposed to wait in Moroski's car. This isn't a great place for you right now. Go back—"

"Dad, I heard a gunshot!" I search again for guns in the Poles' hands. "I thought they killed Grandpa or you."

"Gunshot? It was probably a door slamming. Nothing works right here." He shakes his head. "Damn place. It's alright, David. Go back out and wait for us. Nobody is going to hurt us here. But your Grandfather won't give in. The Polish government let this place go to hell. It's disgraceful."

I'm relieved it wasn't a gunshot, but frightened for my stubborn old Grandpa. He looks like Custer at The Little Big Horn, surrounded by these creatures. "Grandpa, are you okay?" He looks pale, and I don't like him being crowded in by our enemy. What if he has another heart attack? What if they decide to get rid of us like they tried sixty years ago? With all three of us down here nobody would be the wiser. We'd be just more ashes on the trash heap.

Grandpa says to Moroski, "My grandson is here. You talk to the Poles. Get them to pay their rent or leave. I will be back." He walks toward me without his cane. "Why did you come down?" he asks, concern on his face as he leans against a post.

"I heard a gunshot. I was afraid for you and Dad."

"A gunshot? You came because you thought I was shot?"

"Sorry, Grandpa."

A baby girl, held on her mother's shoulder, is blinking her eyes at me and smiling.

I don't smile back. How can I? I thought someone had been shot. All I want to do is get all three of us out of here in one piece.

Grandpa follows my eyes. "You were worried about your Grandpa?"

Dad drops his arm on my shoulder. "Papa, did you hear that? David thought you were shot. Your only grandson risked his own life because he thought you were in trouble. Isn't that enough? You scared the daylights out of your grandson."

The baby is playing 'peek-a-boo' with me. She keeps ducking behind her mother and then popping up again. I can't help it. I find myself playing back. Over and over, she ducks her head behind her mother and then pops up again. She looks like an American baby, only wrapped up against the cold in this basement.

"She's cute, this baby," Grandpa says, his voice softer than I've heard it in a while.

"Did you really shut off their heat?" I ask, seeing the baby is bundled up in a thick jacket, hat and mittens, a bulky scarf wrapped around her neck. I look around and see all the children are wearing thick sweaters and jackets. Some of the coats and jackets look really ratty. I feel the cold myself and realize what it must be like for the children. "Grandpa, please tell me you didn't shut off the heat?"

"David, I have no choice. When you are older, you will understand."

"Mom says, there's always a choice."

"Listen to your grandson," my father jumps in. "At least David has compassion."

Grandpa shoots him a furious scowl. "What should I do, my brilliant son? What should I do with such people who live here and pay not one dime of rent?"

"Why should anyone pay rent for a slum like this?"

"They made it a slum. They're no good."

They're off arguing again. I tune them out. At least they are safe…for now.

The baby is still playing with me. She is all wrapped up, head to toe. Does she deserve to be punished like this? How can I hate a baby? How can I let a baby live in conditions like this? The Nazis could let babies die….

The baby ducks up again, a smile playing on her face. Her cheeks are red.

I stood by and did nothing while Tony clobbered a fourth grader. It took a while before I got the courage to step up. I can't wait that long again. I hope

Grandpa won't be angry. "Grandpa, this baby didn't do anything to us."

Grandpa turns to me, eyes still angry, and says. "You know what they did."

"They're babies, Grandpa. Dad is right. We have to always remember what happened. But do we have to hate those who did nothing to us because they were born German or Polish...just as I was born... half Jewish?"

Grandpa stares at me.

I figured out why he and Nana left New York. "I know you don't hate me," I say to Grandpa.

"I love you more than life," Grandpa replies.

I stare at the crowd around us. They are people, many young. Not one was alive during the war, and we are causing them to suffer. WE, not the Nazis, not Hitler, are doing that to others. Hate is like a disease. It is contagious and spreads out of control. I have to say something. It is the hardest thing I ever said. "Grandpa, I hate what the Nazis did. I hate these people. But please? Turn on the heat? Please, Grandpa? We are better. Do it for the babies? Do it...do it for me? I don't want to hurt anyone anymore." I looked into his eyes. "I don't want you to either."

Dad smiles at me and peers into his father's face. "Did you hear, Papa? You've even made your Grandson hate these people. Is that what you want? Do you really want your Duvidel to think it is right to hurt others? Do you want him to see you like this, to remember you like this...so angry...so uncaring...a Grandpa who made babies suffer?"

Grandpa is silent for what seems a long time. He appears to be studying the baby who is smiling over her mother's shoulder.

I offer a silent prayer, tired of the whole ugly thing. "Grandpa, please? It's enough."

Grandpa wiggles his index finger at the baby, who ducks her head and then pops it up again. "You know, Duvidel, you sound like your sweet Nana. She was one in a million. So are you."

"Grandpa, let's go home? We don't need this."

Giving me a sad smile, Grandpa calls the lawyer over, and says in English, "Mr. Moroski, it is enough. I know what you are doing is to help us. But, please, as my dear Grandson says, it is too much. You will turn back on the heat, the water and the electricity, right away, please." He gazes at me and I see my Grandpa's true face again...not angry...maybe sad. "My Grandson is right. These are human beings." He sighs. "We can't do this anymore. I can't. I am sorry."

I see Grandpa is exhausted. Clue: He is leaning on his cane in front of the Poles, something he swore not to do.

Moroski waves his arms angrily. "You may as well give it away if you give them everything for free. As your lawyer, I am telling you, we can't get them out for months, maybe years, maybe never!"

Grandpa looks uncertain again. "David, you hear what Moroski says—"

"Papa, do what is right," Dad interrupts. "Nothing is worth all this pain. We don't need this. Let's think of them. Please?"

I point to the baby. No matter how much disgust I feel about what the Germans and Poles did to my family, I won't become like a Hitler. "Grandpa, please? I don't want this house. I hate it here. It's not our home anymore. It's hell. Let's go back to our home? Give them what they need. Show we are better."

Grandpa is silent for a long time, and then says softly, "Maybe, that is the answer." He aims his dark eyes at me. "You are right, David. We don't need this. Maybe, I will give them the damn building."

"What?" I don't believe my ears.

Grandpa says, "What else would I do with it anyway? My son doesn't want it. And I can't let children, little babies like this one, suffer because of me. The Nazis took much away from me, Duvidel, but not my heart and soul. I won't let them take that. My mind is made up. End of discussion!"

"But sir," the lawyer erupts. "I've...We've worked years! You've wanted this for so many years! How can you give it away?"

"You heard my Papa," Dad says. "Give them the house. Maybe, it will make some families happy again. We'll show the Nazis they didn't win. Let the hate die here. As Papa said, end of discussion."

It doesn't take a detective to see the frustration on the lawyer's face as he listens silently While Grandpa explains his wishes to the anxious tenants in Polish.

Some of the squatters' faces look surprised. Some men shake their heads as if they don't believe what Grandpa is saying. A few still look angry.

"You did real good," Dad says to me. "At least he listens to you. You can go back outside. It will be okay now, unless you-know-who changes his mind. Then I'll kill him myself." He laughs when he says that, but after all this, I wonder if he's joking.

Yankee has been listening to Grandpa talking to the tenants and smiles at me. "Good," he says. "You, Da-vid…home run!" He laughs and slaps me on the back. "Home run," he repeats, pointing at me.

"Home run." I mime batting an invisible ball out over an invisible ballpark fence.

The lawyer, Grandpa, and Dad, are again surrounded, but now a few tenants have little smiles on their faces. Even the lawyer's face looks less angry as he listens to Grandpa answering some questions.

"It's okay, son," Dad says again, "You can go out and play with your new friend."

I almost snap, "He's not my friend," but nod instead.

As Yankee and I walk back up the dark stairwell, I get dizzy and grab the railing. I didn't realize how frightened I was. My legs are like rubber bands. Was the fear my grandfather felt during the Holocaust something like what I felt when I thought he was shot? I feel so sorry for Grandpa and everybody who experienced this terror. Holding onto the corroded banister, I climb the stairs, grateful when we are again in sunlight.

Yankee jogs back to the alley bouncing the ball in his hand. "Home run," he keeps repeating. "Home run, Da-vid."

I can tell he is happy about how things are turning out and giving me credit for the 'home-run' that hopefully will solve the problem of the building.

I hang back by the basement window. The shouts no longer echo in the hollow street that flowed with hate and blood for too long. That hate, ignited by Hitler, was a disease, contagious, and deadly. Grandpa had it shadowing him for sixty years. After learning how our family was murdered, so did I. It was this undying hate that haunted my Grandpa's face and allowed him to forget his principles, allowed him to hurt others. I don't want to feel that inside me anymore. It makes me unhappy.

It amazes me how these awful feelings don't go away even after sixty years. Like that swastika on my school's walls, the hate keeps coming back to cause more trouble and pain. Will it ever go away?

Yankee calls my name.

I no longer hear shouting from the basement. I hope that is good news.

I take a last glance at this building that looks like a decaying tombstone in the cloudy sky, and head to the alley.

Yankee is smiling, and showing with impatient hand signals it is my turn at bat. For once, I feel like I hit a home run. Is it really over?

CHAPTER 36

Yankee and I take turns hitting the ball. He's a pretty good hitter... for a foreigner. I'm joking. He even stops and gives me a few pointers. At first I'm kind of 'twitchy' when he comes close, especially when he grabs my hands to show me a good grip on the bat. After a while, I appreciate him wanting to help me.

I still listen at the boarded-up windows for the sound of arguing. It's too quiet, like the calm before a storm. It's like in a lot of movies where silence unexpectedly explodes with violence.

Yankee pitches and I miss the ball.

"You must watch ball," he says.

I breathe a huge sigh of relief when Grandpa and Dad come out of the building more than an hour later. Dad is smiling, a good sign.

Mr. Moroski is still talking to the tenants as they join us outside. He has a smile on his face as he shakes the hand of a heavy-set man with dark curly hair and a thick beard, who I guess is their leader.

"Thank you. Thank you. You do good. Thank you. Thank you," this man calls to my Grandfather.

Grandpa waves, but without smiling. "Let's get out of here. I am exhausted," he says, leaning on the cane to help him walk. "I pray I did the right thing."

Dad takes Grandpa's other arm, helping him walk. "Papa, I am so proud of you."

Grandpa grunts. "I don't know if Papa and Mama would approve? But what else could I do? I could not hurt them anymore. It is enough."

"So you're really giving the building to them?" I ask, hoping he won't change his mind. I know how stubborn he can be. I inherited it from him. Remember?

"Thanks to my Boychick here, and you, my brilliant Duvidel, we are working on a plan. No more fighting. It is enough pain to last a lifetime."

I feel the same. I look at Yankee waiting for me. I don't want to fight him or anybody else. Not anymore.

Grandpa smiles weakly. "I think you will like the plan. I will pay for some paint and other things they need to fix this place up decent. And they promise to do most of the work. The lawyer, Moroski, will make up the new owner papers, and soon..." He chokes up, unable to finish.

I see he is fighting not to be emotional. How can he not be after all he did to win back this building?

"It's a good plan, Papa," Dad says, gazing warmly at Grandpa. "You made these families very happy today. You made me happy and proud. It's a new start. We need to remember always what happened. That must never die. But the anger, the hate...it is time to bury them and give hope to the future. I love you, Papa. I love you so much."

Grandpa can't speak. He is fighting not to cry.

I am too. I look at Yankee and wonder again if maybe Dad is right, that we should not hold kids like Yankee, or that cute little baby, responsible for what happened to our family. Yes, nobody should forget it happened. We have to learn from it and work to make sure it never happens again, not to anyone. That is why the memory of the Holocaust must be kept alive. But did Yankee deserve to be punished for something others did? Did he or the other children deserve to live in such terrible conditions because of us?

I understand how Grandpa feels. He lost so much, fought so hard to at least get this one thing back. Now he is witnessing it all happen again... not all, thank God. This time he is giving away his property without being forced to helplessly live the horror of his family being ripped away from him forever...my family. I will never know them. That is the great tragedy of this unbelievable act of human cruelty...so many families needlessly torn apart.

"Papa, it's time to leave," Dad says softly, as if afraid of waking Grandpa from a magic spell in which he has given away an important part of his life.

Grandpa nods and turns back to the building. "Please, God, that I have done the right thing today?"

"Yes, Papa, you did," Dad says, placing his arm around Grandpa's quivering shoulders. "It is time to go home."

Grandpa lets out a deep sigh. "I don't know. I have given away our home, the last memory of my family...all what remained." He sniffles into a handkerchief.

I take Grandpa's hand. "That's not true, Grandpa. This ugly place isn't all that's left. You have us."

Grandpa smiles even as tears fall down his face. "As always, you are right, my brilliant Grandson."

Moroski starts the car. "I think it will be okie-dokie now," he says. "My new American friends, thank you. I am proud to take care of everything for you. It is a happy ending. No?"

Grandpa's lips quiver and his hand grips his cane.

We drive slowly past the small crowd of people who live in our former home. Some are silent, their lips tight with suspicion still, hard to erase after so many years. But a few have smiles on their faces and wave to us as the large black car pulls away.

Grandpa is pressed against the window staring at the building he will never see again.

I can see him crying in the reflection of the tinted glass. I feel it too. It is like saying good-bye to a living creature, one that was dying, but now has hope of coming back to life. I look out the rear window and see Yankee waving his cap and smiling. I automatically wave back.

Dad says, "You made a new friend."

I'm about to answer that he's no friend of mine, but instead I say, "Maybe, I'll send him a real Yankee baseball cap when we get home. I bet he will like that."

CHAPTER 37

Before we went to Poland, I didn't believe in ghosts. I didn't think a place could be cursed. Now, I'm not sure about anything. Grandpa was right. His story changed me, but maybe not for the better.

"Now that you know our history," Grandpa says to me as we're eating breakfast in the almost empty hotel dining room, the following day, "there is someplace I want to show you."

"Is it a surprise, Grandpa?" I was hoping for an amusement park, like Disney World. Two days in this hotel while Grandpa, Dad, and Moroski were working out the details of transferring the ownership of the building with government officials, was bad enough, but there was something much worse: Grandpa and Dad are hardly talking to each other. I think it has to do with the lawyer shutting off the heat, water and electricity to force the squatters to leave. But why would they still be angry?

Dad stops eating. "David, your grandfather wants to show you something that very few American children, or grown-ups, ever see. Honestly, I'm not sure I agree with him," he says, not looking once at Grandpa's face. "Anyway, you don't have to go, if you don't want to. You can stay right here in the hotel and watch television. I can't let him go alone, and it is my one chance to see this for myself."

Grandpa pushes his plate forward. "Your father is right. It is your choice. I want to show you Auschwitz…where I lost them." He pauses. "I must go while I am here."

"A detective is brave" is now my motto. It is a way to pretend I'm not afraid when I really am. I know I don't have to go to Auschwitz, the concentration

150

camp where Grandpa, Nana, and his family were sent to die…but I have no choice. "I want to see where I lost my family," I reply, trying to sound strong. But do I really want to see this hellish place?

Grandpa looks deep into my eyes. "David, I won't force you. I must go see them one last time, but it is really your choice. I would not be angry with you if you decide not to go. I promise."

"I'm going." I have to see it for myself after all I've heard. The story still seems unreal.

"Are you sure, son?" Dad asks. "You don't have to. You really don't."

"Yes, I do." I'm afraid even as I say it.

Riding in Mr. Moroski's long, black car makes me feel like I'm rich, a celebrity. It almost makes me forget where we are going. We drive past the city streets and race onto highways that seem surprisingly like those in America. The roads can almost fool me as to where we are.

Grandpa is silent the whole way.

So is Dad.

I wish they would both not be so 'thick-headed' and talk to each other.

Moroski's driver says something, in Polish, of course, and Grandpa leans forward to see out the window. His face turns pale. "We are almost here," he mutters.

I race my eyes to the window. I'm surprised to see what look like endless miles of fences topped with barbed wire with trees in the background. The trees make it look pleasant until you see the fences which stretch far past what I can see from the car.

We pull into a lot with several dozen other cars and a line of four tour buses already parked. It looks as if we are at an amusement park. There are no roller coasters and happy, colorful, signs.

Grandpa isn't getting out of the car. He grips my hand. His skin feels cold and clammy. "Grandpa, are you having another attack?"

Grandpa stares at the strange scene before us, but still doesn't move. "Oh God," he keeps repeating in a low voice. "Oh God. Oh God."

"Dad, something is wrong with Grandpa!"

My father leans into the car. "What's wrong, Papa? Is it your heart?"

"Yes, my son, it is my heart." Grandpa pulls himself out of the car. "This is the place where the devil took my heart." He takes my hand and I don't pull away.

We are walking between two walls of wire fencing. The barbed wire at the top looks sharp enough to tear flesh to the bone. I don't want to think of what happened to anyone who tried to escape.

"This was the camp to which the trains took us after three terrible days," Grandpa whispers, pointing to the train tracks.

Camp? Concentration camp? I remember reading those words in the computer entry in school. "It's gigantic," I say, unable to see from one end to the other, frightened by the size of it, knowing why it was built.

"So many are here," Grandpa says. "So many."

"Is this where it happened?" I ask Dad.

"You don't have to go in. You can stay in the car. We won't be long."

I stare at the long rows of buildings, many brick, some wood, so rotted away they have large holes in their sides. I don't know what I expected, but these buildings are sad looking, so plain, so ordinary. Is this really the place? Was it here, in this dreary looking barbed wire surrounded camp, that Grandpa lost his parents and his brothers and sisters?

Terror is creeping through my body just seeing the endless barracks and high fences, tall towers where I imagine armed guards watching every movement of the thousands of desperate prisoners. I can almost see the dogs too.

This place is haunted. I feel the ghostly chill throughout my body as where we are begins to fully sink in. This is where the mystery started more than sixty years ago. Is this where it will finally end?

CHAPTER 38

Have you ever seen a movie where the killers are holed up in some awful looking hideout and the cops are outside anxiously getting ready to storm the place? As I stand outside the entrance of Auschwitz, I feel like those cops, only more scared. It's as if the air is different, heavy. I'm breathing fast. *A detective is brave. A detective is brave.* I keep telling myself that, but I would do almost anything not to go through that gate.

"That sign," Grandpa says, pointing to a black sign hanging over the entrance. "That sign is a joke."

"What does it say, Grandpa?" I need a laugh and he said it was a joke. We get closer to the camp entrance. *A detective is brave....a detective is brave.*

"Arbeit macht frei," Grandpa says. "It means, 'Work Makes You Free.'" It was a lie, a vicious, evil, joke."

"I don't understand," I say. There is nothing funny about that 'joke.'

Grandpa looks up at the sign as if he wants to tear it down. "When we saw this sign, we believed it. We believed if we worked hard, we would be free again. That is the terrible joke. They would never let us be free, unless we died first." He hands me his cane. "I will not let the Nazis see me walk with this." He walks under the sign, head held high, even if his walk is more a shuffle than a strong march.

Dad takes my hand. Even though I'm twelve, for once, I don't pull away. Pretending I am a brave detective isn't helping here. I learned too much about this terrible place. There is fear in every part of my body.

"I remember like yesterday," Grandpa says. "Boychick, we stayed some-where in these barracks. Look how many. It was terrible cold. No heat. No

153

nothing. My parents was already taken away. The two little ones…gone forever." He pauses as if he is having trouble going on. "I try to watch over the others. I tell them if we work hard, the Germans will free us. We will all be happy and together again in our own small house." He shakes his head. "I knew it was a lie. The Nazis wanted us all dead."

I shiver thinking I would have been their target too.

Grandpa coughs. "The dust is thick here. My sweet Esther, she was one in a million, died from the asthma she got from the icy cold and the damp. For so many years, she suffered, fighting for every precious breath from the damage this place did to her lungs. We was always cold and hungry. They gave us almost no food…and one after another would die. Nobody would care. Nobody stops it." He stares at the bare wood racks that served as beds, three layers tall. He reaches to touch a bed, but pulls his hand back. "We would sleep two, sometimes three to one bed, like on shelves at home. It was always cold, so we hold each other… but more would die. You never know who is next. I wished to die…so it will all be over."

I can't imagine ever wishing to die. Maybe I would in this place.

We walk outside, toward the back of the rows of brick buildings.

Grandpa is hobbling, but refuses to use the cane. When he stops, I think he is resting, but he is staring at something as if he's seen a ghost.

"Don't Papa," my father says softly, but Grandpa raises his bony, shaking, finger, pointing at a strange-looking chimney. "This is the worst memory of all."

"Dad, please?" My father looks upset, as if he's also seen a ghost.

Grandpa peers into my face. "When will Duvidel see this again, my dear son? Soon all of us old men and women, the few survivors left, will be no more. Who will tell our story if not my sweet Duvidel?" He smiles gently. "You are frightened, my David. It is natural. I am too. But where you stand now is where my life ended. Nobody should ever forget. Nobody should ever think this terrible thing did not happen…could not happen again."

Dad says, "Papa, I know it happened. I've lived with this legacy all my life, day and night. Papa, I hate this place, and I hate the monsters who did this to you. You know that. Can we please leave now? David has seen enough—"

Grandpa interrupts, "I must stay. For our family and all six million Jewish people who was exterminated. For all of these poor souls trapped here forever, I must stay."

I shiver again at the word, 'exterminated.' How do you exterminate six million human beings? I know now. There were death camps like this all over Europe. They were factories of death.

CHAPTER 39

"Exterminated." I hate that word. "Exterminated." Like Jeff's father kills rats or bugs. But the victims here were not bugs or rats. They were men, women, children, babies... millions killed like bugs, like rats, and nobody stopped it. I know now these human beings really were exterminated... hundreds shot after digging their own graves. They were unarmed, defenseless, shot by firing squads and falling into pits where nobody would ever find them. 'Exterminated,' gassed, in the hundreds of thousands...adding up to millions...just like pesky bugs...all 'systematically exterminated,'exactly like the article on the website said. It happened here, and in the unholy network of death camps Hitler set up all across Europe. It was like science fiction, a mad man dooming millions to die for no real reason except his own irrational hate and lust for power. It was impossible to believe, but it happened, not thousands or hundreds of years ago, but in my Grandpa's lifetime. I thought we were better than the cavemen and all the early people who fought endless and senseless wars. Looking at my Grandfather's sad face and his stooped body I feel like screaming, "How could anyone do this to other human beings? They were HUMAN!" I'm fighting not to cry.

Other people walking around are weeping or look sad and as if they're fighting back tears. I've never seen such stern expressions. They hate this place too. But they know they had to come. Maybe, they didn't believe it happened either. Here, you believe.

"David, you see those buildings? That is where thousands and thousands of innocent people was murdered because they was too old, too young, too sick, too weak to work. This is where the monsters killed them...my family... the family I loved." Grandpa coughs and wheezes at the same time.

Dad looks concerned. "Papa, let's go now?"

Grandpa shakes his head, his mouth hidden by a handkerchief. "All that was left was the ashes. There was not even a tombstone, not a burial site. Oh God, how could this be?" He bursts into tears, his body shaking, pounding his fist on his chest.

I'm frightened as Grandpa weeps uncontrollably. I want to help, but I don't know what to say. Dad's hand is shaking as he holds me. I don't want to look in his eyes. I don't want to see him crying too.

"I am sorry," Grandpa says in a creaky voice, eyes raised to the sky. "I should have done more to save you. I should have done something..."

Who is he talking to? I look around.

Dad lets go of my hand and holds Grandpa, trying to sooth him. "Papa, you did your best. You were only a kid, a scared kid. There wasn't anything you, or anyone, could do. It wasn't your fault. Nobody could stop it. Nobody could have saved them."

"I should have died with them," Grandpa says. "Oh God. Why?"

That is too much for me. The tears gush down my face. I can't control them anymore. I fought them for too many months. I have to do something, say something. But what? I feel empty, drained by all I've been through. I want the pain to stop. *Please, God, let it end?*

"Papa, do you think they would like us to say a prayer for them?"

Did my Dad say that? He never prays. He never goes to synagogue. None of us do. Mom isn't Jewish and Dad says he doesn't believe in God anymore. Only Grandpa still believes. But how can he have faith when God let something this horrible happen? It was as if God shut his eyes and ears while all this was going on. Yet Grandpa believes only God saved him when so many others were murdered. It's one more thing I'm confused about. Why would any God let this nightmare happen to innocent people? Not even Sherlock Holmes could solve that mystery.

"Come on, Papa, let's pray?" Dad reaches for Grandpa's hand.

"We should pray in this hellhole?" Grandpa echoes my thoughts, pulling his hand away.

Dad grabs Grandpa's hand again, completing a small circle with me. Through tears in his eyes he says, "Papa, what better way to show the Nazis they didn't break us? Right here, in the deadly 'machine' they invented to destroy us, we will show them that our faith, our hopes, our dreams, can never be exterminated. We will sing out our prayers to show them our family is still standing, still surviving, can never be destroyed."

Is this really my Dad?

Grandpa wipes his face with his sleeve. He closes his eyes and his voice cracking with all the pain he suffered all these years, rises loudly, "Yisgadol v yiskadosh shmay rabah...."

Grandpa told me later he was reciting the *Kaddish*, the "Mourner's Prayer." It is a prayer every Jew, through thousands of years of history, says over the death of loved ones. It is one of the prayers he recited most of his life, alone. He said it every morning, for the family he lost during the war, but also for the son he lost when Dad married Mom, a non-Jew. I now understood this was the real reason Grandpa and Nana moved away.

I don't understand how any parent can stop talking to their child just because he, or she, marries outside of their religion. I couldn't understand how my grandparents could leave me after I was born. But now that I know about how they suffered because others wanted to destroy their religion, I understand why Grandpa and Nana couldn't accept Dad and Mom getting married. I think I could never give up my children but they were tortured and watched helplessly as their families were shattered by hate.

After many heated arguments, Grandpa and Nana left New York, coming back only for rare, short, visits. As much as they loved my father, they couldn't accept their son marrying a non-Jew after what they suffered. I finally understand why Grandpa and Mom always were cold with each other. I also get why my being born added to the pain. Grandpa and Nana must have felt awful I was not going to be raised Jewish.

It seems so unimportant what religion you are when you are free to worship as you please in America. That changes when you understand how others tried to destroy your family because of it. I don't think my grandparents were right to give up on Dad and Mom, and me, but at least now, I understand why they did it. I know Grandpa loves me, even if I am only half Jewish. Nana did too. It was just hard for them to accept. I wish they had. All those years we could have been together.

After so many years of not praying, I'm surprised Dad knows the right times to say "Amen." He signals me and I whisper, "Amen," too. It is strange saying it for the first time in my life, in the middle of a concentration camp, but if anyone hears us, they don't react.

Many of the other visitors have tears in their eyes, are holding soggy tissues and each other's hands. Some of their lips are moving silently. Maybe they're praying too. A few are as old as Grandpa, but almost all are much younger. They could not possibly have been here during the Holocaust, and yet they look like they're crying, or in shock. It is more than just 'seeing,' this place. It is 'feeling' something sinister, from head to toe. I don't know how else to explain it. The evil fills you up.

"Thank you," Grandpa says, wiping his nose with a tissue. "Thank you for coming with me on this difficult trip. Boychick, Duvidel, I'm sorry."

Dad looks at Grandpa and says, "Papa, you weren't wrong. If we let ourselves forget, it can happen again."

Dad said it too? The way he said that frightens me more than anything else I've heard since this whole thing started. "It can happen again." Can it? Even Dad, who is so kind and forgiving, believes it can. Is that why Mr. Hernandez showed me the swastika on the wall? That ugly black symbol of hate wasn't painted sixty, fifty, forty, even ten years ago. Someone put it there overnight. On my school. Don't they know what it means? Can it happen in America? Can it happen now?

Thankfully, we only stay in Auschwitz a few more minutes. Grandpa is tired, refusing to use his cane as he shuffles on the pathways. He mumbles as each step triggers another memory.

Almost nobody we pass speaks. There is no laughter. How can there be?

I learn later there are many rooms and exhibits Grandpa did not let me see that day. Maybe Dad convinced him they are too frightening, or Grandpa was too weak to stay any longer. Soon, we are back by the entry.

I'm glad we're leaving. I hate this place so much. I pray to God a volcano opens up and swallows it down to the fiery hell where it belongs. I feel as if dust is covering my skin and clogging my throat. Is it dust? Or is it the ashes? Is the heavy air my imagination? I don't know. I just know I can't wait to leave.

Grandpa stops inside the gate.

Dad and I are past the cruel black sign, "Arbeit macht frei."

Grandpa isn't moving. He's staring back into the compound with a far-away look on his face.

At first, I think he's having another heart attack.

CHAPTER 40

I want to run to the car. I'll do anything to get away from this awful place that has seen so much suffering. It is evil.

Grandpa is staring at us. Another attack? No sign of pain on his face. He isn't grabbing his chest. Why isn't he moving? A chill rushes through my body. He isn't coming back with us.

Grandpa said he felt guilty being the one who survived when so many others died. Was that why he brought us here? Was he planning to stay in this awful place, the burial ground for the ashes, the wind-swept ashes…all that was left of the family he loved? Was that his plan all along?

Dad explained to me months earlier, "For the survivors of the Holocaust, the 'chosen few' who miraculously lived through it, the guilt must have been unbearable." Grandpa had to face this guilt alone because his son gave up on God and the religion that did not save our family. I was amazed Grandpa did not give up on God, and through all his suffering, did not lose his faith. In fact, the suffering seemed to strengthen his beliefs. He always said it was God and his faith that helped him not lose all hope, even when he lost everything else. I wonder if faith would make me feel better.

As I feel my Grandpa's pain in my body, as if it is my own, I am no longer sure I can give up my religion and God. Isn't that what the Nazis wanted? Wasn't that Hitler's warped dream? Kill every Jew and wipe out our religion so people would only believe in him. It was a sick dream. I won't let Hitler win.

Grandpa is staring back into the camp.

"Dad, he's not leaving," I whisper.

"Papa," Dad says gently, "The lawyer will want his car back."

"They are all here," Grandpa says, as if in a trance. "They are waiting for me."

Waiting for him? I can't leave Grandpa here. What can I do? *God, please tell me what to say to him? Please God?*

The voice comes from inside me. Maybe from my heart. "Grandpa, say good-bye to them. Tell them you love them." I say, wondering if their ghosts are still somewhere in the death camp waiting for him to join them. "Please, Grandpa, we need you. I need you. Say good-bye and come home with me."

Grandpa looks at me, his eyes glossy. "Say good-bye? If only it was so simple?" He looks back, his eyes look beyond, seeing things I can't see...I'd never want to see...images of the past, horrifying pictures no camera can capture as vividly as his mind. He still isn't moving.

As much as I don't want to, I walk back under that terrible sign and reach for his hand. It feels like an ice cube. "Please Grandpa? It's what they would want. They want you to tell me the truth, so I never forget. They want me to pass their story down, so it is not lost in the future."

"David is right," Dad says. "We need you, Papa. They understand that. They want that. That is why God saved you. You must keep them alive by telling their story."

Grandpa lets out a deep sigh. "My brilliant grandson says I should say good-bye to you." He chokes back sobs. "How can I do this? I can never forget you. And now, even though my lovely grandson has never seen your faces, he will never forget you. So you live on. You live on in my dear Robert, and my sweet David, who are both here to honor you... and in my daughter-in-law too." He smiles at Dad. "Christine is a good woman, your wife...like my sweet Esther, who was one in a million."

Dad nods.

I can't breathe. Grandpa's hand is holding mine so tight that I'm afraid for him, the strain on his heart.

Suddenly, Grandpa speaks in a tender voice, "So, until we meet again... soon. Good-bye, dearest Papa, and beautiful Mama. I know you wanted to protect us. It was not your fault. I will always love you. God bless you."

Grandpa wipes his eyes with another soggy tissue.

Dad's eyes are glistening.

I feel strange. It really is as if ghosts are all around us, but I can tell they mean us no harm. I'm warm, the cold chill gone for a few seconds from this horrible place.

"Good-bye, Joseph, and little Marta. I wish I had known you more." Grandpa looks at me. "They were the babies. They never had a chance...to live."

I want to ask him how old they were, but can't bear to find out. How could anyone hurt babies? The Nazis really were monsters I can never understand.

"Good-bye, Rachel, and yes, Daniel. Good-bye Sarah, Ruben, and my beautiful Deborah." Grandpa wipes his eyes again. "And Ruben, my big brother, I forgive you for hitting me when I took your watch to impress the girls." He lets out a little laugh. "You remember that, don't you?"

"That's only seven," Dad says.

Grandfather looks at me, bites his lip, and says, "This is the hardest of all. Good-bye, dearest little brother, David. Do you see my wonderful grandson they have named in your honor? He is a good boy, a wonderful boy. You would be proud."

I feel as if Grandpa is saying good-bye to me.

CHAPTER 41

I'm riding in Moroski's car on the way to the airport. Poland has some beautiful scenery, and the hotel was modern and comfortable. That isn't what I'll remember.

I saw photographs at Auschwitz yesterday of the survivors when the camp was finally liberated. Their bodies and faces were so thin and bony from the hunger and cold, brutal, inhuman conditions. It wasn't nature that made so many people suffer. It was men and women who created and operated these killing machines. Dad was right. No matter how I might still feel about the Germans and the Polish, we couldn't do this to others, not after experiencing it ourselves. Giving in to our prejudice and need for revenge is like giving victory to Hitler and all those who want others to be consumed by hate.

Dad is holding his arm around Grandpa's shoulders.

Grandpa is holding my hand. "I told you, Duvidel...David. Now that you are all grown up, it is not a fairy tale with a happy-ever ending." He sighs. "I'm sorry."

I squeeze his hand. He is right. It wasn't a happy story. It was my family's history with lots of missing pieces, puzzle pieces that were lost over the years. With so many of the witnesses no longer here, some of the history is never going to be filled in. Even the best detectives in the world will not be able to solve this mystery once all the witnesses are gone. "I'm glad you took me to Poland with you, Grandpa," I say.

"David, you are?" Dad asks. "I wasn't sure it was the right thing, so I'm glad you said that."

Grandpa smiles. "Why is that, my brilliant Grandson?"

In the silence of the car I had time to think about all that happened to me in the two years since all this started with a late phone call. It was the most difficult time of my life because I learned things that are horrible, gruesome. I learned things about myself I don't like…things I might never understand. I learned to hate others. "You were right, Grandpa, it wasn't a fairy tale. Not even close. But I'm glad I now know what happened to our family. It's scary, and awful, but we need to know it."

Grandpa says, "I warned you, it would change your life."

"That's why we didn't want to tell you," Dad says. "Your Mom and I just wanted to protect you."

"I know. But hiding from something doesn't make it go away. Now that I know the story, I'm going to tell it to my children too someday. They have to know, so it doesn't happen again." A chill races through me when I say that. "Dad, I want an honest answer, please? Do you think it can happen again? Can it happen here?"

Grandpa looks at Dad and so do I. If anyone can erase my fear and suspicions, it is my father.

Dad looks into my eyes and lets out a small smile. "David, since you want me to be honest, I truly hope it can never happen again to anyone, but I don't know. I honestly don't know."

The End

AFTERWORD

On September 11, 2001, a terrible act of hate sent two airplanes into the World Trade Center, and another into the Pentagon, killing three thousand people.

And the hate goes on…

Dear Friends,

Thank you for reading this special book. The last survivors of the Holocaust will soon be gone. This genocide casts its shadow on families all over the world long after Hitler and the Nazis were thankfully defeated. This story was inspired by the actual reclaiming of a house in Poland sixty years after the Nazis sent its owners to Auschwitz. The characters are fictitious. Unfortunately, the events, the horrors of the Holocaust, are too real. I hope I have not given you the nightmares I had as a child because my parents were concentration camp survivors. Their suffering made me hate prejudice and bullying, and inspired this exploration of hate's destructive, lasting, effects.

Some readers may be surprised David's parents never told him the truth about the Holocaust. My parents rarely spoke about it to us. They may have been too busy with problems as immigrants, and other personal issues, but also I think it was to protect us from the unspeakable atrocities. I know some of you may be frightened by some of what I describe here but I have tried to include as little of the true nightmare as I can while relating some sense of the terrible things Hitler and the Nazis did. David's 'mysteries' are ones with which I, and many others, still struggle. Why would anyone build such a 'Killing Machine?' Why did so many have to die?

I hope this story inspires you to learn more about the Holocaust, prejudice and bullying. I pray I honored my parents, relatives, and everyone, whose lives were sacrificed and shattered by the Holocaust, and all acts of violence and genocide, before and after this man-made nightmare. I believe, "Those who do not know history are doomed to repeat it." I also believe, as Anne Frank did, that most people are good.

Thank you again for taking this journey with me.

NEVER AGAIN TO ANYONE.

Love and Peace,

Mark

Florida, 2021

A PERSONAL NOTE AND APOLOGY

This has been one of the most difficult books I've written, but I had to write it. It is based on true events, but I apologize I had to add parts from my imagination and research. The real people in the story are no longer with us, so much has been lost. I truly regret that and urge everyone who has a story to record it before it is lost forever.

Without giving away too much, a trip to Poland, that is important to the story did take place. Unfortunately, I was not on that trip, so I have to go by secondary sources. As much as possible I researched the facts, and descriptions, but apologize if I've gotten something wrong. I can only say that my objective in writing this book was not as an educator, but as a story-teller, hoping David's story helps children who know nothing about the Holocaust become interested in learning more about this important example of prejudice and hate. It is time to destroy the forces that create the 'killing machines' and build the tolerance and respect that will bring us peace and love. If children learn at an early age what hate can do, we can stop the bullying that is such a problem in America today. This book is about the Holocaust, but also about all hate and intolerance. We must end hate now.

PLEASE SHARE THIS BOOK WITH ANYONE YOU THINK MAY ENJOY IT.
   YOUR KIND REVIEWS ARE SINCERELY APPRECIATED.

More from AimHi Press and Newhouse Creative Group

Visit newhousecreativegroup.com for more books and other products from AimHi Press, NCG Key, and the rest of the Newhouse Creative Group family!

About the Author

Mark H Newhouse was born in Germany two years after his parents were liberated from Auschwitz. He is grateful his suspenseful novel, *The Devil's Bookkeepers 1*, which brings to life the shocking events in the Lodz ghetto, which his parents miraculously survived, won the **Gold Medal Historical Fiction** and **Best Published Book of the Year** from the **Florida Writers Association.** All three books won medals from the **Florida Writers Association** and are receiving rave reviews. Book 3 is a Finalist in the **Eric Hoffer Book Awards** for Historical Fiction; The **Montaigne Medal** for "The Most Thought Provoking Books"; and **The da Vinci Eye Medal** for its cover. A gripping audiobook is now available for Book 1, and Book 2 will soon be released on Amazon.

A retired Long Island, New York, teacher, **New York State Reading Association Teacher of the Year**, Mark, was also an adjunct professor of education at SUNY, Old Westbury. Now, residing in Florida, he is State Chairperson of the Florida Writers Association Youth Program, a member of the Board of Directors of the Florida Writers Association, where he has won more than seven awards for his books. He is the founder of Writers League of The Villages, the Central Florida Book & Author Expo, and the founder and Top Cat of Writers 4 Kids. He writes the *Writing Bug* column in **Village Neighbors** magazine.

His award-winning mysteries include *Welcome to Monstrovia, being developed for film*; *The Case of the Disastrous Dragon*, and *The Case of the Crazy Chickenscratches*, as well as *The Rockhound Science Mysteries*, which won **Learning Magazine's Teachers' Choice Award.** Picture books include *Alice in Batsylvania*; *Passover Puppy Coloring Book*; *Santa's Speeding Ticket*; *A Bite Before Christmas*, and *Dreidel Dog*. All of his books are available on Kindle and Amazon. Please use the contact form at www.newhousecreativegroup.com to order signed books and learn more about Mark.

Mark, a former Long Island resident, received his BA and MA from Queens College, CUNY, and Administrative certification from Hofstra University. He lives in Florida with his very patient wife. Thank you for your kind support and reviews. Hear Mark present "Taming My Monsters," free at Daniel Pearl Education Center: Mark H. Newhouse, on Youtube.

You can connect with me on:
 https://www.facebook.com/MarkH.NewhouseAuthor

Also by Mark H Newhouse

The Devil's Bookkeepers Series
Book of the Year - Florida Writers Association
Association Royal Palm Literary Awards!

Never again to anyone.

This is a story of love and courage in the face of unrelenting terror as four men in the Lodz Ghetto struggle to document the tightening of the noose under Nazi rule.

Written by the son of Holocaust survivors, this stunning novel based on events described in the Chronicle of the Lodz Ghetto (Yale University Press, 1984), asks what you would have sacrificed to be one of the few to survive.

"What Ann Frank's Diary did to put a face to the plight of Dutch Jews in WWII, The Devil's Bookkeepers does for the Jew in the Lodz ghetto," **Rita Boehm, Award-Winning Author**

www.ingramcontent.com/pod-product-compliance
Lightning Source LLC
Chambersburg PA
CBHW071603180626
46819CB00002B/113